W9-AAB-067

The Mermaids
in the Basement

The Mermaids
in the Basement

—— STORIES ——

Marina Warner

Chatto & Windus
LONDON

Published in 1993 by
Chatto & Windus Ltd
20 Vauxhall Bridge Road
London SW1V 2SA

A CIP catalogue record for this book is
available from the British Library.

ISBN 0 7011 4623 0

Designed by Humphrey Stone

Phototypeset by Intype, London
Printed and bound in Great Britain by
Mackays of Chatham PLC, Chatham, Kent

FOR ESTELA WITH LOVE

Acknowledgements

The author would like to thank Roy Porter for advice on the historical background of 'The Food of Angels', and to acknowledge the inspiration of Joan Jacobs Brumberg's study *Fasting Girls* (1990), where the case of Sarah Jacob is described. The following stories were published earlier in slightly different form: 'Be My Baby' in *Serious Hysterics*, edited by Alison Fell (1992); 'Mary Takes the Better Part' in *Cosmopolitan* (1983); 'Salvage (After Tiepolo's *The Finding of Moses*)' in *New British Writing*, edited by Malcolm Bradbury and Judy Cooke (1992); 'The First Time' in *Loves & Wishes*, edited by Antonia Till (1992); 'Ariadne after Naxos' in *Quarto* (July/August 1982); 'Now You See Me (After Veronese's *Susannah and the Elders*)' in *Firebird* 3 (1984); 'The Legs of the Queen of Sheba' in *The Fiction Magazine* (April 1987) and *The Best Short Stories of 1987*; 'In the Scheme of Things' in *Storia* 3 ('Consequences'), edited by Kate Figes (1989); 'Full Fathom Five' in *The Fiction Magazine* (April 1985). 'Heartland' was broadcast in a different form as *Seductions*, on Channel 4 (1991).

I started Early – Took my Dog –
And visited the Sea
The Mermaids in the Basement
Came out to look at me –

EMILY DICKINSON

Contents

I MOTHERS & SISTERS

Be My Baby   3

Mary Takes the Better Part   21

The Food of Angels   40

Salvage   57

II HUSBANDS & LOVERS

The First Time   85

Ariadne after Naxos   97

Now You See Me   121

The Legs of the Queen of Sheba   137

III FATHERS & DAUGHTERS

In the Scheme of Things   163

Full Fathom Five   180

Heartland   195

I

MOTHERS & SISTERS

Be My Baby

The blanket was the standard issue white cellular sort they wrap babies in, and I could look through the holes though nobody could see my face as I was coming out. The pinpricks like stars with people in bits behind them made me think how it was when I used to go to confession and Father Sylvester was just a shape behind the screen like a ghost, though in this case I was the ghost, that's what I looked like in the photos the press went on taking just the same, though all you could see of me was a white blob, a Hallowe'en prank, with the police around towering over me, they were old-fashioned in their height, I wondered about that. I like a tall man, I like to feel little. Andrew used to call me his little chickadee, his baby bunting and sweet pet-names like that and though he isn't exactly a big man he had a nice pair of broad shoulders on him, and I could make him feel really big, you know, inside me, he liked that about me, that I could get him so excited he'd shout he could shaft a horse. I could see the mouths of the pressmen opening and shutting, they were calling out to me, wanting to have a good peek, but I wasn't going to let them, what was in it for me? Besides I don't give myself away to just anybody, like Sister Richard used to say, save up your treasure on this earth and you'll lay up more treasure in heaven. And we all know what she was talking about. One-track minds, the nuns, in spite of their sheltered life.

Near the courtroom, one of the police, it was the woman detective, she held on to my arm, really tightly, she was hurting me – and I was already hand-cuffed to her. She was walking me fast into the build-ing from the van saying I'd have to tell my story later, most likely, but not yet. I could see more mouths opening and shutting through the gaps in the blanket. I didn't hear what they said, though the words thumped me inside like when I bring someone round from a heart attack, making my pulse race and a leaky feeling deep down, like fear but not as nice as the big dipper when it plunges and your innards go all melting. Because it isn't true what they were saying. I love my baby girl, and I know how to look after her really well and I did look after her, there wasn't a spot on her, she was bright-eyed and bushy-tailed when they found us and took . . . and that's a right sight more than you can say about half the mothers I see around me on a daily basis.

'Rowena isn't the right woman for me,' that's what Andrew said over and over, I know he did. I should have been having the baby instead of her, it was his unspoken thought, I know it was, I could always read his mind, he was easy and I could feel how unhappy he was. Of course, then everything could work out for the two of us, I saw it, instantly. I like Rowena, she's good fun, especially when she's a bit oiled, and she's that often enough. I sympathise with her, she's got a problem, who hasn't? She's the frigid sort. We call it vaginismus, I told Andrew, we get patients in all the time with it clenched tight like whelks. You can warm a speculum as long as you like, and coax them, Relax relax, you can massage their tummies and even stroke the inside of their legs, but you can't get it into them, no way. Anyway Andrew says that when he does get it in, he feels like Napoleon marching to Moscow and it's about as cold and bleak and – I shouldn't say it – huge in there as the steppes of Russia in winter. These poor women who are past it, one minute they're so tight, the next they're gaping, no control. The vagina walls all slack. I mean, Andrew says that as soon as she was pregnant she wouldn't let him touch her breasts any more, not that she's got much to offer in that department, and she wasn't exactly overgenerous in what she allowed him before. It hurts, she'd say. Well, that's not much of a turn-on, is it? I couldn't tell her, Sweetheart, he fits me to a T. I gave her a tube of gel and told her to hire a video. It was really peculiar to be counselling her how to get off on her own husband specially seeing as he's a real tomcat when it comes to me.

Conjugal duties, we were taught about that. I remember Sister Richard putting a question to us: If your husband was suddenly posted abroad, to India for instance (I can't think how she'd think anyone'd be going there, more like the other way about, they all come here, England's still a great place, even though I switched to private when I started working for Andrew in the clinic, nothing can beat the National Health). So, if your old man's off to India, do you go with him or do you stay behind and look after the children? Well, I think most of us girls answered, Stay behind for the kids. Being mothers was the big thing, after all, they were always drumming that into us at the convent, the Good Lord gave us the equipment so we could have babies. Not just for fun, young ladies. No way. That's right, I still think that. But it turned out that we were wrong. Sister Richard pointed out that our duties lay first and foremost with our husband, we had to follow him to the four corners, never mind the kiddies, leave them in a home, or preferably with Nan, because otherwise your man's immortal soul will be at risk, occasions of sin everywhere, all those invitations to the flesh issued by natives, the females of the species in their gaudy getups with their funny smell like curry – actually Andrew loves curry, the hotter the better – you had to save him from that. Otherwise you'd become a kind of occasion of sin yourself, by omission, like not waking up to a patient's bell the first time and finding when you do get there that you're too late and she's lying in a pool of urine or worse and so ashamed she tells you she wishes she'd croak and couldn't you help her. I think the geriatrics had the same effect on Andrew as on me. He said something about the front line of decay and death, about nature

6

asserting herself to preserve humanity. Anyhow
Andrew sometimes has to push me up against the wall,
or over a table, or once up against the drug cupboard
just as I was getting out some Temazepam for one of
the old dears who'd had a bad night. I never had time
to put the bottle down but had it in my hand throughout, he was that urgent.

I had to lift the blanket when I got into the court, but
the magistrates had cleared the room, so there was just
me and them and the police – and, yes, the lady solicitor, and it was funny, because first they charged me
with something and then she objected to that because
that section of the law had been repealed, she said. A
right muddle. Anyway then they got the right law and
the right section and the right offence according to
their way of thinking and hers and they all looked
pleased as Punch saying that I did take without lawful
authority or reasonable excuse a child under one year
from the lawful control of her mother and her father. I
saw red when I heard that, I know the kind of people
Opal's so-called mother and father are, the idea that
those freaks are lawful and I'm not is just a farce, but
my lawyer said I really couldn't talk, that I'd have a
chance later, at the proper hearing, this was just com-
mittal proceedings. I'm still waiting. Meantime I'm
stuck in the bin with a whole lot of perverts and sex
maniacs and I'm certainly not going to give any of
them the time of day, however much the doctor says,
Let's include Norma, or asks me if I have any thoughts

on the subject in hand. I've got plenty of thoughts, I can tell you, but I know that doctors are clueless most of the time and they'd be lost without Sister to tell them what to do, so I'm not going to fall for his tricks, and certainly not in that company. One of the men is a – I can't spit it out – no better than an animal and one of the women who was giving us her life story yesterday with lots of bawling – crocodile tears if you ask me and a bid for attention – she's a pro and she's been one since she was twelve years old and her mother put her on the game. Well, I felt a little stab of sympathy when I heard that. Typical, I thought. But I wasn't going to let her past my guard, because if you have a mother like that you're lost from the start. I could feel sorry for her, but she's still rotten right through to the core, might as well have terminal cancer for what her chances are, and the rot would've set in irreversibly when she'd have been about three. I used to worry about my little girls, my Susan and my Mandy coming back from school on their own, I used to warn them about men making approaches, I'd feel an idiot talking about sweets from strangers, but the things you read in the newspapers about vice rings made me scared for them. Mandy was such a pretty little mite with her fair hair I used to do for her in a French braid. Maybe that's why she's working in a salon now I haven't seen her since she was . . . well, she's grown up now, she's left the home where they placed her. It was the best, the bedrooms were newly painted she said when she phoned me one time. That's when I had to go private and start night shifts, after I'd given Evan his marching orders because I'd had it up to here with him and anyways that was what I had to do, everyone said so, it was better for the kids too in the long term than to be growing up with a brutal father who'd bash you soon as look at you when he's fed up with the night's viewing on the telly. There comes a time when you've had enough –

It's down to the mothers, just the same. That's our burden, and our glory. Andrew admits that Rowena's feeble, and it's no good, if you can't say boo to a goose you certainly can't cope with a kid. Mothers are a lousy lot and getting lousier, I think you'll agree, I said so to my lady solicitor, and she asked me to go on, she was taking notes. She was listening and nodding, she probably comes into contact with dreadful people, seeing as the law deals with criminals and perverts . . . not always, of course and in the medical profession there's a few normal people around and the old dears, of course, they're not in the clinic for anything we can't talk about. Though I've had some crazy times, sometimes, that's another story. Mothering's a skill that's in decline, I told her, like home cooking and turning collars and darning socks along with the graceful old dances like the quickstep and the waltz which we were taught at the convent so that we'd have all the accomplishments young ladies need to keep a man happy. She took it all down on her yellow pad. Dreadful handwriting, lucky I'm a nurse and can read anybody's scrawl so I could see she was making extra notes about what I was telling her. Not bad but mad? Not bad but mad? she had the nerve to scribble and think I wouldn't understand. I just laughed at her. I'm biding my time.

At first I wasn't sure about the underwear, it made me giggle, the knickers with the bit between the legs cut out, the 'love gusset', the label called it, the bras with holes for your nipples to poke through. Andrew left this Valentine mail-order book for me with a really sweet note, he said, 'For my baby bunting, with a big wet kiss from Daddy Bear' no name of course, just in case, you never know who's snooping around, and at first I didn't want anyone to know about us, because, well, he didn't want to hurt Rowena, he's a decent man, and she was having Robert and she was getting on and he didn't want the baby upset either. Impressions in the womb count, he's right to be careful, it begins before birth even, the influence of the parents.

He was always saying, 'There's the baby to consider.'

In the last place where I worked I had my tubes tied, I'd never told Andrew that, didn't get a chance to, we had better things to talk about than my medical history, I can tell you, but after the three kids I felt enough is enough, it seemed right at the time, and Evan was ever so keen, there was the one I'd lost too. The girls were growing up so we'd have to split them from Sammy and put him somewhere else, in the living room, or in with us again. The council kept on saying we'd be rehoused, and when I started working nights it was hard to get the kids off to school on time they were in such a mess without me around to clean up. I know the Pope says it's wrong to have your tubes tied, and I see why now, but the girls we have in at the clinic for the D & Cs could do a lot better if they went the whole hog and got sterilised, then they wouldn't be killing their babies after they're formed, all perfect in miniature I've seen them on the spatula. And I mean when you see the little thing wriggle on the sonar scan and you can even spot its willie if it's a boy it's a right sight different from shedding the ovum before it's fertilised I think, I don't like working on terminations but I have to hand it to them these patients at least admit they're no good at being mothers, which is more than most of the ones walking around with dozens of kids already and another one in the pipeline.

I asked about getting them untied. It's not like a vasectomy, though. Men have all the luck, lucky devils I say they are, even in something like this, snip snip, they're back to normal, but in my case, no go, what's done's done.

At Christmas Andrew had the office party in his house. I encouraged him, it'd be a real treat for all of us, and I told Rowena we'd all be on good behaviour, I'd see to that, I'd keep the little SENs in line, no spilt drinks on her new shagpile, no rings on the french polish. It was really fancy, outside catering, tree on the lawn, nothing routine like multicoloured fairy lights, no, all in silver, with snowflakes like stars lit up. When

Rowena tucked up early, she was tired, she was near full term and almost everyone had left and those that hadn't were past caring, we had a secret session in the sauna room, it was really erotic slithering on the wooden slats, slapping around with the towels with the steam hissing and then the cold water, whoosh, like a rush of amil, it was straight out of a video. Andrew that night wasn't like a man of fiftysomething, I told him, he was a young billy goat, honest. Then he was lying quiet. I love him more like that, when he's almost like a baby, and I stroked him and dried him and helped him back into his clothes again and combed his hair, and he was all tender and docile, like a patient who gives no trouble to the staff and I knew I had to make the decisions for us. Men are like children, everybody says so, but that doesn't stop it from being true. They can't take a step without someone holding them by the hand, That's right, put it down there, now there, well done, until they can crow, Look, I'm doing it, all by myself. So I thought, Andrew can give us a good home, more than Evan ever could, I shouldn't have even tried to make a family with him, but I was young then and I was clueless, I admit it. But now, now that I've got the full benefit of experience, I can live my life again, I mean men are always doing it, getting married and messing up and then starting again. The kids are grown up now, Susan's got a bloke already, Mandy's in the salon, Sam'll be out of school soon into YTS, they have programmes now for school-leavers better than in my day, and I'm only thirty-eight. I've got my whole life still ahead of me, I said to myself. I'm free to choose a new one. That's what I'm telling myself, lying there on the boards in the sauna with Andrew like a lovely big baby who's had a really good feed lolling against me all blissful-like with a little smile twitching in the corner of his mouth, which may have been the beginning of a snore, just like an infant who's not really smiling, just having a bit of wind and the silly mother goes all cooey and gooey because she thinks a baby of ten weeks already knows how she's Mum and is smiling at her for special.

Some of these mums beat belief: I stop now and give them a really good stare so that they can see that someone is paying attention to their carry-on. You'd think children were as hard to handle as a Tornado fighter plane the fuss they kick up in public to win sympathy and attract attention, the way they crash and go up in flames at the least opportunity, yanking at their kids and shouting blue murder. Well, they don't get my sympathy, but I notice. I'm building up a file on your little lot, I feel like saying. Only I don't, I keep quiet, biding my time.

You can break the new mums down into several sorts: there are the whingers, the ones who go snivelling along behind their pushchairs, saying I'm at the end of my tether I haven't got the money for another Ninja turtle I might have tomorrow if you're good. Then there are the glamourpussies, the ones who hang about together smoking with their long red nails glinting checking their gloss lipstick contours in their compacts while in the pram – this lot always have the fanciest cabriolet-style navy blue and gold jobs with four-gear suspension – the toddler is choking the baby, sitting on his face or beating him up and meanwhile Mum's puffing away passing the time of day with her friend, Dick this and Ron that and Franny this and Myra that. Do you really think women like that deserve to have kids? And I won't even get on to so-called one-parent families who invite child abusers right into the bedroom and say, Yes, sweetheart, go right ahead, bugger my baby, stick your finger right in there, doesn't that feel nice. God, I sometimes wonder if You still exist or whether the redemption has run out, like money in a meter, it's nearly two thousand years since God so loved mankind He gave His only begotten son to die for us and maybe the effect is fading. Sometimes I felt that I didn't have the strength to keep on loving enough to hold me and Andrew and Opal together, when he didn't come and visit us that time the way he said he would and didn't call until the next evening and then muttered about things had come up at the clinic and he'd got held back in the office, I was a bit upset, I had to summon up all my energies to push down the bitterness I felt swelling up inside. But I was just sweet to him down the phone, I didn't want Opal to hear any disagreement between her father and mother as she was peacefully lying in her cot in that halfway state babies lie in, with their eyes open, looking but not looking, must be the way our consciousness is when we're bodiless, like the saints in heaven.

Of course, Opal isn't bodiless, and I take care of all that side really well, even the people in the town when I went out commented what a beautiful baby she is. I called her Opal because it's my best birthstone, I was born on November 22, feast of Saint Cecilia, that's why I like music, Sister Richard used to say. Opal and me have the radio on often, we go dancing together, that's how I describe it to her, bobbing up and down with her against me to Marvin Gaye or someone with a tender sweet singing voice like his.

I laid up a really beautiful layette for her, nothing but the best, took the coach to London one Saturday I had off, before Opal, but when I already knew, knew as certain as day is day and night is night that the time was coming when I'd have her all my own, and I went into the White House, Bond Street, W1, which is the place for baby clothes since Queen Victoria, I was calm as you please and asked for a recommended list of layette items, the shop assistant was very accommodating. Madam, she said, and showed me the newborn section, because she could see from my shape I was soon due. There's this linen romper suit with écru smocking Madam and mother-of-pearl buttons so I pointed out to her that these'd dig into a baby's flesh when she's asleep. She was showing me more from a drawer behind the counter and displaying them for me in a pile on the glass top there were so many, she said nuns in Portugal embroidered them, they still had the nimbleness in their fingers to do tiny details and the patience of course as well. It wouldn't have been good for someone who didn't know to have the romper suit the way it was, and when I got home I cut off the buttons and put nice flat poppers instead and it was such a lovely hot summer that when I put Opal in the stroller with the lace parasol I picked up in Mothercare and she was wearing her romper suit with the écru smocking so that her sweet soft knees with the dimples in them peeped out, we stopped the traffic, I'm telling you, and that's not easy in this country where most everyone behaves like children were a bad smell under their noses.

Andrew was a bit surprised when I told him about the baby, but he gave me some money – he's a real gentleman when it comes to the open chequebook – and he was pleased I found a cottage in the village so quickly. I've got good stomach muscles I told him, when he was investigating, they just snap back like suspenders I said. Rowena was still baggy, I could see him thinking, I can always read his thoughts, seven months since baby Robert was born and she hasn't recovered her shape such as it was. I bought flowers for the little table in the window nook and made chicken vindaloo with real crisp poppadums the way he likes and Opal was good as gold in her Moses basket. He said she had a very nice-shaped head, which is true, I wouldn't have a forceps delivery, even a low forceps, I know what that can mean in the long run. No, Opal was born full of the joys of spring, easy birth, four hours after the waters broke, no epidural even, I made sure by reading the notes on her because I couldn't remember anything myself, not afterwards. The notes were in the babies' changing room, one of the nurses left to answer a call and she had them with her. I remember talking to yet another of those taffyhead girls – another single parent, of course – who'd just let the world roll over her and brought a baby into the world without knowing one end of her from another. All she could talk about was her stitches itching and the size of her boobs and the milk flooding. Opal was lying on the changing mat waving her arms and legs and I knew she'd be better off without such a person, rabbiting on about herself instead of dedicating herself to the job before her. She hadn't an idea what it meant of course and I didn't see it as my task to straighten her out on the subject. I was going to care for Opal and give her my full attention.

There was a nice cot with Furry Forest Folk painted on the headboard in the Mothercare book and I hadn't managed to get a cot, you can't wheel one out of the shop like you can a buggy and bring it home on the bus, so I showed the picture to Andrew and he said, Go ahead, and he wrote me another cheque for a bit over the cost of the cot, and I almost came over funny, because he was committing himself to us, when Opal got to be the right size she was going to sleep in a bed chosen by me and paid for by her father and it was only a matter of time, I just had to be patient and loving and I'd be requited in full measure. Like the nuns used to say, still waters run deep and the mighty shall be cast down and the meek shall inherit the earth.

It would all come to Opal and me in the end because we deserve it.

I caught the news on the telly with a Photofit that didn't look in the least bit like me and I saw the girl and her boyfriend pretending to cry so that they could screw some money out of the papers and the fool public who come over all soft when they see tears in a so-called Mum's eyes. I hugged Opal really tight and put the radio on and got a Golden Oldies station and I danced with her holding her close and it was one of the sweetest times of my life – someone, was it the Ronettes? – they were singing all these sweet nothings and I repeated them softly, singing along with them, Oh yes, she's my baby, my very own, baby now – and I was never never ever going to let her go.

I really never expected to be so happy not ever ever it was like a big light shining inside me and setting me all aglow to have Opal mine to care for and bring up right. I went to mass with her in the snuggly – I hadn't been for a long time but I wanted to talk to Our Lady and all the Saints and Baby Jesus and I'm telling you I got down on my knees to say thank you for Opal's life and mine and Andrew's and to pray to them to give us all a chance to thrive together. Thrive is the word, 'failure to thrive' that's what people say about children with the wrong kind of mothers, Evan kept on repeating it to me one time I remember after one of those meddling council people'd been at him again.

The doctor at the therapy group asks me if I've got any

more feelings about Our Lady and her being on my
side. She was a single parent, too, he says. Which just
shows how much he knows his gospels since her marriage to Joseph is written down there plain as day. I
told him in no uncertain words. Then one of the perverts said that I was an unmarried Mum myself with
Opal if you accepted that she was mine in the first place
which she wasn't and I tried to break in and stop his
dirty mouth but the doctor let him speak and he went
on – he's an inarticulate brute stumbling over his words
as if his teeth didn't fit under his lips and he said that
Andrew couldn't have married me for ages seeing as he
was married already and the quickest divorces take a
year so that technically I was a single-parent family
too. I shot him down in flames. That's what it might
be 'technically' I said, but what does love have to do
with 'technically'? He said, You're really confused, and
the doctor then shut him up which was about time.
But I was upset, they were driving a wedge between
me and Opal and between me and Andrew and that's
when I asked the doctor if I could have the blanket
back so that I didn't have to see them all except in little
bits and pieces which makes them manageable the way
you just uncover a portion of the patient's body during
an op so the surgeon can work without being disturbed
by stupid distractions happening elsewhere.

He protested but not very strongly and asked the
nurse to bring me one, and I feel much better now
wrapped up with everything that's not inside my head
muffled and screened off. There was a paper in the

corridor with that idiot girl on the front – she should be making toothpaste ads – and the headline was like the doctor but saying more loudly that Opal was her baby and I had to go along with it.

But I know she's still safe and warm inside with me, she sucks the corner of her white blanket when she's hungry and I'm preparing her feed. I always use the thermometer to get the temperature just so and change the steriliser water more often than the instructions say, even though they're only keen to make money out of babies and don't really have their health at heart.

I know the smell of her apricot soft skin and her little wet mouth like a rosy sea anemone – Sister Richard used to say the nun's was the highest calling, but that motherhood wasn't far behind.

Mary Takes the Better Part

I found the broken plate in the cupboard. I was stacking too many dishes on top of it and I heard the crack. It was a clean break and the plate was porcelain, always easier to mend than earthenware – its grain is so fine. There was a little heap of other things to stick, a teacup handle, a brooch with its clip off. So I gathered up these bits and pieces, and, spreading a newspaper on a chair in the kitchen, began mending.

I like glue. I usually use quick-drying, but the last time I was in the ironmonger's the young man told me slow-dry was more reliable, and I took his advice. The tubes and their tops were colour-coded, the boy pointed out, so that I shouldn't stick the wrong tops on the wrong tubes after using them the first time. His fingers were like spanners, flat and square; his arms were as strong as jemmies, with the sleeves of his overalls pushed up and a name bracelet 'Darrell' showing.

I squeezed out equal amounts of the white and then the yellow, and mixed them with a match. The glue coated the end of the little stick immediately in a viscous cocoon. The plate was a pretty, scalloped one my father had given me. It's painted a beautiful cobalt, with birds of paradise in the centre in rose and green and freely decorated in gold around the edge. It had broken in three pieces, cracking from the centre where the dishes had weighed on it. I smeared the edges and brought the two larger pieces together. They made contact, but there was a rift; I pushed the opposite way; the rift became a hairline. The glue oozed up under the pressure.

The way china fits, even after a break, is so satisfying. It's a surprise to me, too, each time that it does so, that there hasn't been any loss of chips or powder, that, even while breaking, the integrity of the object somehow remains, undiminished. And that's not something that you can fake, I thought as I squeezed the plate. (With the slow glue, I soon realized, you need patience; the tackiness that makes mending with rapid epoxy a race against time takes longer to develop.) I sat holding the pieces as tightly together as possible, waiting.

A friend of mine recently shattered her elbow. She'd been to a keep-fit class and was showing her daughter how high she'd learned to kick. But she was demonstrating in the kitchen, and her foot slipped on the tiled floor. Down she came, crushing her elbow. They found all the bits in her arm, but an elbow is not like a plate, and she now keeps all the pieces they couldn't fit together again in a jar on the kitchen shelf. They don't look in the least human, more like dried mushrooms.

The crack was slipping about a bit when I added the third section, even though I tried to hold the pieces

22

steadily. I couldn't resist trying to press them a little harder, to make the hairline itself disappear, and then I'd overdo it, and the plate would suddenly jolt out of joint and I'd have to slide it back again. The mend was firming up at last, when the phone rang.

It was my sister Mary, and of course she wanted me to come over and help her. (She rarely rings up for any other reason.) 'I've got a proper patron coming. Honest. Please.' She'd asked him to supper. She hardly ever boils an egg herself, yoghurt and wheat crackers being her staple.

The trouble is that Mary's appeals work on everyone, not just on me. She's so openly helpless, you can't fail to feel genuinely and desperately needed. And there's something pleasurable in resisting the natural resentment her demands inspire. She paints a halo round your head.

'I'm sticking a plate,' I said. 'I'll come when I've done it.'

'Thanks. Soon.'

There's another thing. I get a kind of glow from the way Mary makes me feel capable. 'Can you pick up some food on the way?' There was a pause. 'I'll pay you back.' Another pause, as my disbelief made itself felt down the line. 'I know he'll bite, especially if you make one of your delicious fantastic super delicious meals. *Please.*'

It was already six on a Saturday night; but there's a luxury deli that stays open near me as well as the corner shop where new sell-by dates have been stuck over the

23

old ones, and so I went out and bought some smoked bresaola and anchovy-stuffed olives, two pounds of spinach and cheese tortellini and some cream and mushrooms for the sauce, a quarter of grated parmesan, some ready-washed *mâche* and rocket salad greens, and – irresistible – a large frozen packet of blueberries at a terrible price. But I couldn't say no at the sight of them, so firm and dusky blue inside the frosted plastic bag. I was just about to pay, when I remembered that Mary never has sugar either, so I had to go to the corner shop after all and dust off a bag. That I really resented; it was double the price of the supermarket. Blueberries from Vermont are one thing; but white sugar!

But I was looking forward to the meal, to making a show for Mary and her patron. I wanted him to yield, to fold his hands over his well-fed stomach, sigh at the treats I'd set in front of him, eye us both with appreciation and . . .

A few years ago – it must be getting on now for ten – when Mary was leaving art school, I remember there was a queue at her Diploma Show stand, and the notebook she'd left dangling on the table next to her swatches and albums of designs was chock-a-block with neatly printed messages from representatives of fashion houses. She was soon selling her fabrics everywhere; and then she was bought exclusively by some huge firm. She was jubilant at the time, they were giving her her own collection, and her trademark – a stencilled columbine – would appear on the selvedge of all her materials. Most fabric designers never have a name at all, they get swallowed up, I remember her saying.

Before she joined the firm, Mary used to dye her own lengths herself, or paint directly on to cloth. She never produced any piece of fabric that was more than – I don't know – enough for ten garments. She treated lengths of stuff as individual works, like sculptures or paintings.

The company gave her one collection; she complained that the colours did not reproduce her patterns, and the cloth was inferior to the quality she had stipulated. She was told that it was uneconomic to produce a fabric in one colourway only; she had to make the same designs work in at least six different schemes, and look as different as possible, so that the machines could print at a profit.

After six months, she heard that a factory that the company owned in the north was being closed down by them. 'Uneconomic', of course. It was a family business, going back hundreds of years, she said (she was absolutely distraught, and I wasn't going to pick her up on facts). They were the finest weavers of silk left in the whole world, with secrets that even the Chinese had forgotten.

'They can spin a single unbroken thread for 100, oh 150 metres of cloth, heavy as linen, and if it breaks once, only once, they set it aside as seconds. I'm telling you, their seconds are like . . .' She was jawing in her distress.

'. . . Like angels' drapery?' We exchanged smiles. We share a love of angels, since travelling round Italy together years ago, and I felt a rush of feeling for her, as sometimes happens to me. I thought, She's my younger sister, we're two of a kind really, and she wants me to help her.

The quarrels between her and the company got worse; and her next collection failed miserably – from the commercial point of view. Artistically, they were as inspired as ever, sumptuous, glinting, like the wings of Saint Gabriel or Saint Michael we'd seen in mosaic in Ravenna.

'I can't work there any more, I can't.'

'But you'll not get another deal like it.'

'I must leave them. They're brutes, and philistines. They don't give a shit for what really matters.'

'But how will you survive?'

'They're the ones who think of money all the time. I'm not going to become one of them.'

'But that's the way it is, now.'

'I'll manage somehow, you'll see.'

If she'd left earlier, she might have found work elsewhere. But she stayed on and things got worse and worse in the textile business, while her reputation for being difficult, for unreliability, for being hopelessly scatty spread through the trade. There was some truth in it, too.

Then she went to Madras. She had a plan that she could help the Indians and begin working again herself in a way she wanted if she designed cottons for villagers to dye using traditional vegetable dyes and then print, too, using their ancient woodblock techniques. It was a good idea. But Mary is not gifted at organisation.

Madras was a year ago, and since then her outgoings, acquired in more stable and prosperous days, are weighing on her.

When I arrived, the flat was in a worse state than I expected. Mary was sitting up on her stool at her drawing board frantically scrubbing with a rubber at a sheet of paper that was well past any prime it had ever had. She'd scarified the paper to a blotting surface, and around her were bundles of samples and trailing clothes and trays with old yoghurt cartons and teaspoons congealed in them, and cuttings torn from magazines and art books open at Titians and Guercinos. (As she gets older, her taste is moving on, too; she'll probably start doing Fragonards soon.) She stumbled down from her perch, almost falling towards me, wringing her hands. Her fair hair was pinned up on top of her head with two pencils, and the sole of one espadrille was lolloping off.

I haven't got Mary's looks, I know, and I learned early on to make up for comparative invisibility with competence. She is tall and straight-limbed and she wears her usual disarray like a costume; a missing button on her blouse looks intended, I've always been able to see that. But I can't produce the same effect. I always sew buttons back on.

'You're a real saint,' she said, pulling open all the

paper bags. 'Tortellini! How delicious. And blueberries! And cream! And sausage! Oooh, *wunderbar*.' She squeezed my arm. I began trying to clear a space for working on the counter in the kitchen. There was a towel hanging in the sink. I was transporting it towards the bathroom, which lies through the bedroom, when Mary came scampering after me, grimacing silence at me, and no trespass.

'What . . . ?'

There's somebody in there, she mimed back, beckoning me into the living room again. 'It's Geraint; he's got someone with him, she's doing her nut about something.'

I tried to listen. 'Are they . . . ?' Mary shrugged. 'I don't think so. At least he came out five minutes ago and it didn't look like it. He said they'd be off soon, but that she was coming on strong about something and he . . . well, he'd got to calm her down.'

I rolled my eyes heavenwards.

'Honest, Martha, they're not at it, I promise.' She giggled. 'There'd be more noise if they were.' She has a kind of laughter that's terribly hard to resist. But I sliced into the tortellini packet with a vengeance and ripped it wide. I turned the tap on to gush and filled Mary's largest pan and slammed it on a gas ring.

'The last thing you want is your new big white hope turning up and finding there's some kind of orgy going on.'

'Oh, Martha,' Mary pleaded. 'Don't be cross.'

'I shan't cook!' I shrieked. Everything was being

spoiled, I could just see it: Geraint suddenly tumbling out of Mary's bed, dragging a girl with tears scorching still on her cheeks, and they'd gatecrash the meal and dominate the evening and no one would pay any attention to Mary's plans or to my efforts on her behalf.

'I couldn't borrow some money? Some more, I mean,' Mary broke in on my swoop around her workroom, as I gathered up stray books, stray linen, stray ashtrays.

'There's some,' I said, pointing to a heap of change spilt on one of Mary's ledges. She hadn't got any wine, she said.

'But there's champagne in the fridge. I saw it.'

'That's Geraint's.'

Mary then promised me that the man who was coming to dinner – he might bring a friend, too, she added inconsequentially – was really bona fide. I shrugged, and gave her my wallet.

The presence of Geraint and his friend behind Mary's door was making me fussed. I'd started the water for the pasta far too early, for one thing; it was seething and would have to go on again when everyone had arrived and had a drink. I tried to sort out my plans, and began washing the salad.

Geraint told me once that I had beautiful feet. Feet! Still, I liked the way he looked at them and made their shape in the air. He has big, reliable hands, which is strange as the rest of him is rather whippety. 'They say there's a touch of the tar brush,' he said once, and pointed to his eyes: 'The dodgy eyes, you know.

Gyppo eyes.' They're so black they're almost blue, and long, and one slants more than the other.

Mary always says to me that they got to know each other too well for sex.

I cleared away the débris that cluttered the table where we would eat, and began laying it. When Mary came back, she dumped the wine in its bag beside me and handed me a corkscrew. 'Let's start, why not?' she said.

Geraint's eyes are also like some kind of dark stone with a star in it, a ring you try to gaze through to find the exact depths at which the rayed light is dancing and discover that you can't, that it keeps sliding away from your attempt to focus on it. But he doesn't really give an impression of gypsy shiftiness, just of quick wits, readiness of spirit. He's sparky. I'm the first to be impatient with contemporary notions of fly-by-night romance, the on-the-road cast of mind, the wonder of the non-marrying man who treats the little ladies rough, and then in the morning, So long, and what did ya say your name was?

But Geraint isn't quite like that, even though I know – witness the scene going on now in Mary's bedroom – that, yes, he is like that. He alights, suddenly, and he's elusive about his whereabouts. He regards knowledge of his comings and goings as a sacred preserve. It's impossible, even for Mary, who is closer to him than anyone in the world, to pin him down for a specific day. He has keys to her flat; she'll find him there, on her couch by the window, with his own travelling rug over him, suddenly one morning. (The rug is rose cashmere, with a long soft fringe of darker pink and a band of the same woven into the border. Geraint carries it with him in its own envelope of leather. It was a gift, of course.)

He lives in what he can keep in his large, carefully tuned old car. But everything he owns is beautiful. That's one of the many things he and Mary have in common.

I have a theory, based on those two: when you've been beautifully made yourself, like Mary, like Geraint, you only feel at ease with objects made to an equal standard of loveliness. Everything Mary surrounds herself with, once you prise it from under the flotsam of her daily disorganisation, has been carefully and considerately fashioned by a particular, confident imagination at one time.

She and Geraint give each other presents. Geraint comes to stay, bearing an old ivory-handled toothbrush from a market stall and a bottle of bleach to soak it in; Mary at the same time has bought him an old comb, of ivory too. But, in her case, she doesn't throw in the bleach. Geraint knows how to look after things.

I remember the best exchange they made. It must have been six years ago; I was still living with Mary then. Geraint arrived. She told him to hide his eyes. Her own were shining, and her high round cheeks were bright on the bone. 'You'll have to find it,' she whispered, spinning him round. 'Somewhere in the room, there's something special for you.' Geraint let himself be turned and turned. 'All right,' cried Mary. 'You can look now.' He stumbled from dizziness, half on purpose, and his eyes scanned the room, shyly, playing along with the child's treasure hunt she'd prepared. He walked cautiously, as if the room itself might change and the present suddenly disappear. He hunted. When he saw it, he didn't dare assume it was for him. Mary noticed too. 'Go on,' she said. 'You're hot, you're scorching. OOOhh.' She fanned him wildly from her perch on the stool by the drawing table. But he went on, afraid to accept it.

'Colder,' I interrupted.

Mary came over to him. 'It's yours.'

She put it in his hands. It didn't look like much, just a battered old leather case. But Geraint flushed. It was an old flute case with a velvet lining of dark blue silk velvet, special compartments for each section of the dismantled instrument, and an oval label in copperplate on the inside of the lid. He put his nose in it and sniffed. 'Fantastic!' he said. He took his own flute from his flat modern case out of his bag and set it nestling in the velvet. 'That's the best resting place you've ever had,' he told it, and he took Mary's arm and squeezed it. 'You are very, very kind,' he said.

She laughed. 'It's perfect for you, isn't it? I knew I had to get it for you.'

Then he showed her the battered box of paints he'd bought for her. There were tears rolling out of her eyes from laughter.

I once went to bed with Geraint. The next day, Mary

said, 'He's not right for you, he'll make you miserable. He's so undependable. You like everything straight, predictable and steady.' She was chewing her hair and looking out of the window as she said it. But it was true, I have to admit.

The doorbell rang. 'Here goes.' Mary pressed the buzzer and called down into the mouthpiece, 'Come on up, first floor.' She waved crossed fingers at me.

I waved back, the same.

Her possible patron was a neatly made, sunburned man in a linen suit of Italian cut, wide at the ankle and pleated at the waist; his skin had a waxen sheen, so that altogether he looked doll-like. He kissed Mary on both cheeks; she was taller, and as she bent down to receive his pecks, a strand fell from one of the pencils skewered into her hair and across his cheek. I shook hands.

'You don't look like sisters,' he said.

'Don't you think so?' I replied softly, unabashed by long experience of this reaction.

Robin Quarles had brought two guests with him. 'Family Hold Back,' I mouthed at Mary, counting out in my head the number of tortellini among the five of us. There was a young woman in a freshly ironed pale blue cotton blouse with a starched dicky front that emphasised her breasts like a nurse's apron. The other man had a familiar name; later I realised that he had once been a well-known milliner. I assumed the girl had come with Robin; the milliner had that soft-bodied look gays sometimes have in middle age. He effused over Mary immediately. One hand waved across the room, indicating the sheaves of designs and bundles of cloth I'd tried to stack more tidily. 'What industry! What imagination!' he exclaimed. Mary poured them some wine – a Verdicchio. I approved.

Robin nodded. 'Oh yes, Mary's got real talent.'

She laughed. I think, like me, she sensed some reservation in his tone. She then led them out to sit on the balcony.

The balcony was a good idea, I realised, because then they wouldn't see Geraint come out of the bedroom with the girl. If he did. I just hoped one of them wouldn't want to use the bathroom before he decided to emerge.

So I dashed ahead, as Mary led them through. I hadn't tidied it; when I got there, some tights and underwear were pegged on the washing line. I hastily plucked them off and clutched them to my chest as I let the others pass by.

The balcony is leprous, the plaster curls up under the eroded paint like bark on an old tree; the pilasters of the parapet are in a state of ruin. It didn't exactly offer the right seating to someone turned out in a starched white dicky. Robin looked doubtful as well about sitting down beside Mary where she perched, over a twenty-foot drop to the pavement below. His suit didn't look the kind to thrive on such dilapidated seating, either. They hovered, the starched girl was saying it didn't matter, but I hurried to find some cushions; Hamish, the milliner, followed me, asking if he could help bring out some chairs.

Eventually they were settled with their glasses of wine, the endangering parapet empty except for Mary. As I left them, to put the water on again and slice the sausage for the first course, I saw how she looked, with the warm-toned light of the evening sun on her bare arms and legs. Beautiful. She'll fix them, I thought to myself. I really wanted it.

When I joined them again a little later with a bowl of olives, Geraint was there. He was sitting on the parapet, quite unconcerned, opening the champagne. The atmosphere had palpably warmed. Hamish had crossed his legs in spite of his bulky frame, and was leaning forward, holding a glass towards Geraint. The young woman was flushed above her snowy front, touching thighs with Robin, who now had Geraint's girl next to him on his other side. She turned out to be, I realised immediately, an actress famed for her disasters. She wasn't a patch on Mary, though. You could see the ravages of experience in every pore, poor thing.

She was nice, though. She had a quick, easy laugh and a fetching catch in her voice from smoking incessantly and an alert manner that took me by surprise after the endless scandals about drugs and whatnot. And she was interested in Mary.

Mary giggled. 'I don't know where I get my ideas, really. Sometimes I dream them. Colours and textures and patterns, rainbow fabrics falling, like when there's a heatwave and you fill the sheet with air and let it settle softly and coolly from the tips of your toes to the top of your head.' She went on. I'd already heard these

35

dreams. Once, she'd found herself at a fashion promotion for 'Nudity, The New Thing'. All the other
designers there were desperate to find some way to
clothe their customers while keeping their fashionable
nakedness intact. Mary had had a brainwave: people
had to wear something out of doors in the winter, so
why not design wraps, made of a single drape of
beautiful cloth, that you could take off when you came
indoors and use as your personal cushion or bedroll or
chair cover. 'In my dream, I'd already made them.
They'd be useful here, wouldn't they?' she said, patting
the peeling balcony. 'Clothes just right for heaven!'

I noticed that the actress had the mark of scratches
on her uncovered shoulders. My breath slipped a gear,
and I looked at Geraint's hands.

He had relinquished the champagne bottle; he was
leaning forward, gesticulating and laughing. His eyes
were glittering. I caught something about a perform-
ance during which the music scores had been switched
and one half of the orchestra had started with one piece,
the other half with another. He saw me looking at him
and stopped himself. 'Martha!' he exclaimed. 'Hello!'
The mischief in his face turned to affection.

I smiled back. You have to admit his vitality. You
can't stop it bathing you all over, as if a cloud's passed
and left you standing in the light.

Then the girl in the starched dicky gave Geraint a
look. It was a look straight at his mouth. Her eyes
seemed to twitch at him like a rabbit's nose. I thought
to myself, So that's how you do it. I stood up with a

jerk, in the middle of something Robin was saying. Then I apologised for interrupting, which made the interruption worse, and then, even more flustered, I announced I was sorry to leave them, but I had to prepare things. The brouhaha soon resumed. The olives I'd brought out were a mistake, perhaps. They always give a thirst.

I set two more places at the table, and started melting the butter for the mushrooms, then heating the cream through for the pasta. I was using a bowl balanced on a pan so as not to scald it. I wished they'd come in and look at Mary's work.

When they didn't, I went out again and asked them to the table. There was a pause, then no movement. I exchanged a glance with Mary. 'It'll spoil,' I said.

Geraint was in full flow; the milliner and the starchy girl were bobbing at his side, like tugboats hooting a flagship's return. The actress was silent now, glancing at her nails and flicking her fingers now and then, waiting for his attention.

Geraint looked at the table, then at his friend, then at Mary. 'We must be off,' he said. 'You're about to eat. We can't stay.'

'Oh do,' I entreated.

He shook his head lightly, and went over to Mary and kissed her on both cheeks.

'You're coming back?'

'Later.'

'Why go, then?' The milliner's laugh was light, but

37

forced. The actress hovered at the door. It was clear she wanted Geraint to herself.

But you could feel our hankering, and its tide pulled more strongly on Geraint than her will, and he spread his hands, shrugged, and said, 'Why not, it looks delicious. Martha's a tremendous cook.'

Everyone laughed, we were all delighted.

They talked and ate; I served.

In the kitchen, between the pasta and the salad, I hissed at Mary, who had wandered in after me, 'Can't you help a bit? I'm doing everything.' Geraint was behind her. He was looking for more wine.

'Martha,' he said, 'Martha, you worry too much! You worry about everything. And there's only one thing that's needed, and Mary knows it.' He mussed Mary's hair with his free hand, and walked over to the table with the wine. 'Enjoy yourself!' he threw at me over his shoulder.

Mary shook her head but smiled, and said nothing in my defence.

And I thought, I will walk to the middle of the room and I will take my clothes off. Then they will stop talking and look at me. I shall display the incandescence that they do not notice. I will look white and whole and polished, and my limbs will be strong and delicate and there will be wings sprouting from my shoulders, made of eagle feathers and swansdown with coloured pieces of stone and glass glinting in them. My feet are beautiful. I will have no weight or cracks or lines. I'll be a pure being, made of light and colour and lightness.

Every one of you'll be able to see then that I'm more beautiful than you inside and that's why I have to keep myself concealed. I could blind people. You'll come to understand that Mary shows everything she has, that there's nothing more to her, but that I am good, so I keep quiet. My waters are still, they run deep. I'll show you all this, and more. Only you're all still talking and eating and laughing. I'll bring out the cantuccini and the blueberries and I'll go on smiling while you nibble at the delicious burnt almonds and burst the tender fruit in your mouths and I'll go on smiling, happy that I've brought you such good things, and under my smile, in my mouth, too, you know, there's hidden this brightness that would take you aback. I could let it show, but I must choose my moment.

The Food of Angels

'Let Love, being light, be drowned if she sink.'
The Comedy of Errors

East Anglia, 183—

LUCY: Meg was there last time we were picking the potatoes, we were all off school for the week, teacher gave permission because everybody's needed at that time. She was quite near me she had no stockings on and I saw her legs all the way up to the top when she bent over, she's fat and her legs are fat too, white and grey and loose, like suds after doing a wash in the tub, and she didn't look as if she felt cold, though the clay was hard with the winter coming, which is why we all had to go out and help so the harvest wouldn't spoil, get bitten by frost and turn the tatties soft, so Da was saying. I saw her underneath too, she had hitched up her skirt as if she'd rather dirty herself, not her clothes, she had hair there I saw it, like another face kind of smiling in a not-smiling way, showing its gums, and with a scraggy kind of beard. Mama says she didn't

40

know what she was doing, God help her, she was simple, that's why she got a baby but I know she ate potatoes. Potatoes make you heavy and fat and when there's too much heaviness and fat it has to fall out of you like –

AGNES: I'm almost as big as Lucy even though I'm two and a quarter years younger and I can swing for just as long as she can from her favourite branch. I'm scared sometimes but it's a nice feeling, tickly, up and down my arms and back. It creaks when Lucy swings on it, she swings really hard. And then you just let go and – whoosh – you fly through the air and land on your bottom. Lucy showed me how, she made me take the hay from the haystack for us to fall on, she said nobody would stop me, she's bold like that. She knows things, she says she'll tell me.

ABIGAIL PERSIS: Our Lucy's a funny girl, hard-hearted maybe, though she'll bleat like a newborn lamb about some matters – you can't fry a bright, fresh pair of kidneys without her choking and looking fit to be sick. She refused – and without a by-your-leave either – to come and see the new baby. Though I told her that God has His plan and even when the rhyme and reason of it stay hidden from mortal eyes, we must accept and love one another as he loved us. Agnes took Lucy by the hand and pulled her away with us, but still Lucy dragged and would not come. She said she hadn't her boots on. She was making up one excuse after another.

I'm sorry to have to say it but I think she's priggish, and unforgiving. That's no way to be in this vale of tears. We're all of us sinners, I remind her. I tell her we must accept all of God's creatures, halt and crooked, deaf and dumb, for, as the Lord said, 'The mighty shall be cast down.' It's the simpletons that will enter the kingdom, when all our betters go down to the other place and roast.

That poor Meg, she's a half-wit, and who knows who put her in the family way? (Though I have my ideas.) And to think that nobody noticed until the birth pangs started and she was on the kitchen floor clutching her tummy and moaning. Then, and only then, did her mother realise. You'd think she'd have had eyes in her head for her daughter's condition. I suppose she thought Meg was safe from the attentions of the gallant sex – she must be half-witted too, but with a difference – being that unsightly and soft in the head as a rotten turnip. Meg still didn't understand what was happening to her, her mother told me, even when the baby was halfway there. She looked happy about it, though. Crooning to it and saying, What a beautiful boy you are, you are. Her mother was looking pleased as Punch to have another baby in the household, her first grandchild, I suppose you could say, in a manner of speaking. She's motherly, she'll take him over, and in Christian charity, one must thank the Lord for the family's carefree ways. That poor idiot girl might have killed the baby by ignorance, if not by other means.

Still, ignorance is innocence and innocence is godly.
But tongues will wag, and, as I say, I have my ideas.

MR LONGWORTH, Fellow of the Royal College of Surgeons: In what terms can we describe or explain living
matter? When we observe the reaction of two chemicals introduced into a test-tube, are we observing life?
No, merely the agency of one substance upon another.
What then do we say when these same chemicals, resi-
dent in the living human organism, react in the same
manner? Is their activity without life, though the body
they inhabit lives and breathes because of these same
agents and reactions? What difference can be ascer-
tained between the action of oxygen upon the blood as
it courses through the heart and the action of oxygen
upon inert matter? No, some other principle differen-
tiates the life of a man from inanimate matter.

Some learned men have proposed that the vital principle resembles electricity, others that it be a fluid, too
subtle to be observed or identified. But I prefer to liken
this vital principle to magnetism, which appears to
animate a bar of iron without forming or altering any
of its parts. Thus a bar of iron may be considered like
animal matter without life . . . Although when the last
trump sounds St Michael will weigh souls in the balance, I put to you that the spirit of life inheres in the
body in an immaterial fashion, that the soul cannot be
weighed. It is life, and life does not possess substance.

Life is light; the soul is light; the divine image is
found in lightness.

LUCY: After school one afternoon – we were coming back along the lane and we ducked under the hedge where there was a gap into the rectory garden and Meg followed us and we pulled from one end and pushed from the other and she was laughing all silly and happy with it though she got scratched on her arms from the briars because she didn't know to keep her arms by her sides and she licked the blood and said she liked the taste of it, it was like spinach. Then Jude said, 'Let me try', and she squeezed her scratch till little beads of blood stood out and he drew his tongue along it. The sun was out and there had been a shower and the drops were shiny on the leaves of Mrs Carstairs's vegetables which were growing there in tidy rows in the rector's garden and some of us were pulling up the carrots and eating them dirt and all, not me, I didn't feel hungry. Then Jude saw a caterpillar curling and uncurling in the dew on a spinach leaf. He calls to Meg, 'Look, a big juicy caterpillar eating the spinach.' Jude was making noises, smacking his lips, and then he was picking up the wriggly caterpillar and making believe he was going to put it in his mouth, his eyes dancing, and dangling it to tempt her. I went along with it, I was laughing too, I said, 'Yum, yum, Meg, nothing nicer than a big juicy caterpillar,' and she said, 'Give me, give me, I want to try it too.' She's so greedy she'll eat anything, and she did, she took it from Jude. I was egging her on – with the others, I wouldn't have on my own – as she chewed it up, working her jaws as if it was rolypoly. And she didn't even spit out one bit of it. No, she laughed after she'd swallowed it and said it didn't taste like spinach or like blood at all. She still looked all moony with pleasure. Then we ran away and she couldn't keep up with us, 'cause we can run much faster than her.

MR PERSIS: The rector preached a fine sermon today: 'Cast thy bread upon the waters,' he said. 'For thou shalt find it after many days.' The Lord in His wisdom will see that it returns to you, multiplied, in greater quantities than before. 'Be ye not men of little faith,' he said. I do have faith. I know that the Lord watches over me and over my house and over my wife and my daughters.

AGNES: Lucy puts her dinner in her drawers when Mama isn't looking. When I saw her she clenched her teeth at me to tell me to keep quiet, so I didn't tell, not anyone, and I promised I shan't ever.

ABIGAIL PERSIS: Mr Persis is reading *Revelations of Divine Love*, by a certain lady in the old days, he calls her Dame Julian, and says that Julian was a woman's name in those times. The rector lent him the book and he's very taken with it. She lived not so very far from here, she's our own, he says, our mother, he says. So to speak. She lived behind a wall, for years and years, occupied with nothing but prayer and the love of God, and nothing but angels and the Lord to keep her company. She was a soul in bliss, he says. On earth, too.

It's not my idea of a happy life, but I don't like to contradict Mr Persis in these matters, and the saints can't be judged by our lights, I suppose. The squire has asked Mr Persis to visit poor Meg on his behalf and give her a half-guinea for the baby – handsome of him. (He did not do the same for us when Agnes was born, but then, seeing Mr Persis is his factor, and respectably paid for it, I suppose he considers there's no need in our case. Still, I mean to say.) The squire was dallying on the path, it seemed to me, he was making enquiries about Mr Carstairs from my Caleb, that's Mr Persis (he likes me to call him so, as the gentry do). The squire was asking about the rector, if he was well. I was glad I'd taken down the cross Mr Persis put on the shelf above the hob in the kitchen. I think the squire doesn't quite like his rector having 'enthusiasm' – that was the word he used. 'All this enthusiasm,' he said, 'what d'ye make of it, Mrs Persis, what?' No more thoughts for Meg and her baby. She's calling him Abel, it's a good name.

LUCY: Agnes told Da that I don't eat even though I told her not to tell and twisted the skin on her arm one way and the other till it burned to make her promise not to. She said it just came out she didn't mean to tell, because he was talking about Dame Julian and how she didn't need the worthless rubbish of this world to keep alive she just burned with the love of God and like a flame gave out light. So Da came and asked me questions. I didn't say anything about Meg and her baby.

The Food of Angels

AGNES: I didn't tell about Lucy putting her finger down her throat at the bottom of the garden. She coughs it up like Kitty when she has hairballs.

MR PERSIS: I have heard of such miracles and Reverend Carstairs agrees. Among the saints, he says, the condition of 'holy inanition' is called wondrous – *mirabilis*. Our Lucy has been chosen. It is a sign of God's special providence. I have written a letter to the newspaper in town to spread the good news that the Lord has seen fit to bless this house. And not this house alone! Our stark fenland, too, where once the prideful men of the Commonwealth did commit many uncomprehending outrages against the true fellowship of saints. Their progeny who call their blasphemies Dissent, as Mr Carstairs tells me, continue the work of the fiend in our own time. My letter will give readers to understand the falsehoods they preach; as our wondrous Lucy is our witness!

ABIGAIL PERSIS: My Lucy's all skin and bone and sits at the table refusing good barley broth and hot bread and when I try and coax her – I don't force her – Mr Persis lays a hand on my arm and says, 'Mrs Persis, the Lord is watching over us. Let her be.' The rector's been to visit too and then they withdrew together into the lane and talked there. They didn't even want to stay in the warm out of the spring winds off the fens that can pierce workclothes even when I've oiled and waxed them.

But Mr Persis was all flushed with excitement, says Lucy's a special girl with the mark of the holy on her.

MR PERSIS: The peasantry live like pigs in a stye and yet we must not abhor them, but see in them the image of our sins and reproach ourselves for the iniquities we behold in them. Yea, verily, as the Lord said, 'Forgive them for they know not what they do.' Brothers and sisters, mothers and sons, fathers and daughters grossly lie together in filth and stifling air. Mankind is not like stock, you cannot breed thoroughbreds from a single bloodline, No, rather the idiot's curse passes on to Meg from Meg . . . Ah! I have warned my daughters of the corruption and dangers of this world, the noonday devil and the others who walk by night.

'From sin, from the crafts and assaults of the devil;
from thy wrath, and from everlasting damnation,
Good Lord, deliver us.
From all blindness of heart; from pride, vain-glory,
and hyprocrisy; from envy, hatred, and malice, and
all uncharitableness,
Good Lord, deliver us.
From fornication, and all other deadly sin; and from
all the deceits of the world, the flesh, and the devil,
Good Lord, deliver us.'

Oh, our entreaties were heartfelt, as we recited together till we were comforted. Lucy's face glowed as she said the words with me, the light of the godhead truly seems at times to play upon her countenance and her limbs. I think sometimes that she might be an angel come amongst us to save us from the corruption that enmires us round about. Dame Julian learned from the Lord, 'Sin is behovely, but all shall be well and all shall be well and all manner of thing shall be well', through the flowing of divine love in us, Amen.

AGNES: I made Lucy a daisy chain with some butter-cups though they don't last at all and I put it on her head for the visitors, and Mama added a ribbon, a cream satin ribbon, she said it made her look brighter in the cheeks. She sits in the chair in the kitchen that used to be Da's and she smiles and nods when people come to look at her. Sometimes they push messages into her hand and she smiles some more she doesn't tell me what they say, but Da collects them and puts them in a box under the cross which the rector has brought to us.

LUCY: Sometimes I'd be tempted, which was bad, and then I had to eat and I'd come downstairs and the wind's fingers would be working in round the door and the windows in the dark of the night and I'd have to hunt I felt like one of the horrible heavy owls outside dropping to the earth all of a sudden to snatch meat. But I'd sick it up before the meat could weigh me down and now I've no weight, it's a feeling I can't explain – it's light, all through me and around me I feel I could float up softly like a dandelion clock in the sun when you blow on it and all the whirligigs lift up into the light –

ABIGAIL PERSIS: I don't know, I really don't, it doesn't make sense to me that a growing girl sits and sits and smiles and smiles and has no energy for anything. She'll dwindle away to nothing, it's beyond my understanding. The doctor's been – Mr Persis was quite upset when I fetched him by – but the doctor says the rector and Mr Persis are right, that it's a miracle my Lucy can live like this on air. It'll be the death of me, I know, I see her just fading away in front of my very eyes and looking so happy about it too, almost as if she was a young girl in love, it's more than flesh and blood can bear, honest to God. But what can I do? It's so hard to tell Mr Persis, he's that distracted, that I've had to buy more tea than we drink in a month of Sundays with all the comings and goings and I've been baking enough bread to feed us for weeks and it's gone. I'm not going to put out the jam any more since there's no fruit yet to make up another batch and sugar's very dear. But when I bring such matters up, Mr Persis says, 'Cast thy bread upon the waters.' Well I'll cast my bread upon the waters, with a collecting box at the door for the gawkers and the gawpers at my Lucy.

DR MEDLINCOTT, Fellow of the Royal College of Physicians: Some learned opinion would have it that because the vital principle cannot be prised out of the animate organism by the dissecting blade on the surgeon's table, that there must needs be an explanation from the world of spirits. This tribe of animists would find that all the powers of inorganic nature have been invoked in vain, and that they must consequently maintain that the soul is the one sustainer of life. But such wilful and empty syllogisms can only deepen the ills in which the modern sciences of physiology and biology at present founder. We cannot expect to discover the true relation of things until we rise high enough to survey the whole field of science and observe the connexions of the various parts and their mutual influence. There can be no life apart from matter; there can exist no vital principle that does not inhere in natural processes. The limits of our present ignorance impede our full understanding of these connexions, but exist they must.

I shall demonstrate it; I shall furnish proof.

MR PERSIS: The rector has brought to visit our dear Lucy one Mr Longworth from the University who is most interested to observe her. There is a most heinous heresy abroad, they inform me, that denies altogether the life of the soul and with it, though I scarcely can bring my mind to bear on it, the Lord himself and his providence for each and everyone he has created in his wisdom. Our Lucy brings back on earth the saints of old: a child who has never known evil is an unblemished spirit. She lives like an angel without sustenance of this world –

LUCY: Some of my visitors want to touch me but my skin's on fire with the light and it hurts me where their flesh touches mine, like a spill flaring when Da holds it out to the flames before lighting his pipe. I lie in bed now, upstairs by the window and I can look out at the light there. The edge of the earth glows too, much more brightly than I ever saw before, it feels like its skin's on fire as well. Yet all the material heavens look dim compared to the brightness in me. The visitors leave me gifts and messages – Agnes comes in after they've gone and she shows them to me but I let her keep them, the things of this world are like worms and caterpillars in my sight. The rector says it is wonderful how I have no desire for the trash and dross of this earth –

DR MEDLINCOTT: I've attended to this new report of yet another Fasting Girl – and indeed Lucy Persis whom I forthwith visited does appear to live and breathe without partaking of any food or drink; yet this flouts the laws of nature (which are one with the laws of the Creator) and there must be some subterfuge, in which she is abetted by the family and the villagers. We will soon discover it. I urge that a 24-hour watch be placed in the young woman's bedroom, and no one else beside the nurses accredited and approved by men of science be allowed to enter. We shall soon see her appetite return and be able to refute foolish notions about the vitality of the soul independent of the body. Then we shall have our proof.

MR LONGWORTH: I have examined the entire family and reviewed the matter with the rector, too. Mr Carstairs has known the young woman Lucy Persis since she was born – indeed it was he who christened her – and I can vouch, with his approbation, that the parents are good people, he a loyal and diligent servant of the gentleman who employs him as his factor on the estate, and a man of indisputable piety and upstanding morals, she a goodwife, who shows less acumen and conviction than her spouse but is prompt to follow him and obey his wishes, as is fitting in a helpmeet. The daughters have been raised strictly, and discipline was not spared in order to mould their spirits to the Christian way, Mr Persis told me. Lucy is a devout young woman, who has been singled out according to the Lord's mysterious purpose for this destiny. She will shine with the radiance of His grace throughout the watch Dr Medlincott desires to place to test her truthfulness, and I am confident in the Lord that with His help we shall expose the blasphemies Dr Medlincott sees fit to proclaim to his shame and the disrepute of science.

DR MEDLINCOTT: I must be allowed to feed her with a feeding tube, or the young woman will not live. She is failing. She has been without food and water now for 36 hours and her limbs are already cold, her pulse very feeble. She is very weak, weakened by hysterical self-starvation over the recent period of several months, and the vigilance we have placed her under prevents her access to those means of sustenance she used before. She must be permitted to resort to whatever means she indulged, else I cannot guarantee her survival.

MR PERSIS: Doubt and disbelief, contumaciousness and pride – the sins of Lucifer are committed by these new men who deny the soul!

AGNES: I used to sleep with Lucy in our room and sometimes when she was very cold she'd ask me to come closer to warm her. Her bones were all sharp, she was like a bundle of knives. Now I'm sleeping with Mama and Da: Mama groans a lot and shakes the bed and Da doesn't come in till very late. I hear him praying loud for Lucy and giving thanks that the Lord has marked our home with a special mark, that's Lucy –

LUCY: I saw Meg and her baby out of the window. She was holding him in the lane, and pointing up here to my window. I could see his round white face just like hers, like they were both made of dripping, and I moved quick away from the window so she wouldn't reach out and touch me with her eyes.

ABIGAIL PERSIS: The doctors want to take her away from here – at least that Dr Medlincott does – but I can't let our Lucy be poked and prodded by strangers far away from home. No, I said, if you're going to examine my daughter, you can do so in her own bed in the presence of her family. He begs me to make her eat something but I tell him that coaxing or scolding or any means of persuasion will not effect a change in her resolution – she only becomes more obstinate if you draw attention to her fast. Mr Persis says she has the strength of the martyrs in the arena – a grace beyond human ken.

MR PERSIS: They want to make our Lucy eat, but I told them you can't do that without making a hole in her. I'm not allowing anyone to take her away and make a hole in her. It's my bounden duty towards my daughter to prevent such an outrage against God's providing.

LUCY: Light light light light light! Piercing me like the sun fullface like the flash of clay after the wet like the eye of the candle flame like the bodies of the angels on the ladder I'm floating on upwards up up up to clouds of glory above where there will be transparency and more lightness, more more!

DR MEDLINCOTT: The coroner's report finds traces of faecal matter in the lower intestine; then, running from the armpit along the left breast, a shallow indentation, marked by an even contusion somewhat like a phial in shape; the lower limbs wasted, from lack of use, and the whole cadaver emaciated as a result of the patient's refusal to accept food. The last time the patient was taken out of her bed to be placed on the scales, she weighed 5 stone, 6 lb. The time of death was given as 6.16 a.m. on Thursday April 23, when the pulse, which had been very feeble indeed for 36 hours, finally halted. I put it to you, Mr Longworth, that the bruising and shallow depression under her arm were caused by an object pressed close to the flesh over a prolonged period, an object like a small nursing bottle, for instance, from which she was taking surreptitious sips to quench her thirst. As for the faecal traces, they speak for themselves. I regret the young woman's death and the enthusiasm of her father and others that contributed to her folly and confirmed her in her self-delusions. However, I hope that the materiality of the vital principle has been demonstrated and that you will accept this case as proof. Human life cannot exist without the body. I do not speak of the soul's immortality – that is an article of faith – no, I speak against lightness, for life is substance and consubstantial with phenomena science can observe.

AGNES: I used to straighten her pillows and smooth the sheets under her and give her a little suck at the bottle because she would gasp at the air as she slept like a nestling and she was like one in her transparent skin and bones poking through and sometimes even when there were people in the room I could give her a kiss and pass some bread I'd chewed up just like a mother bird. That's how I got the idea. She was in the sight of God, she said, but she still couldn't see Him clearly, her eyes were dazzled by all the light, she said. At the very end they wouldn't let me into the room any more and that was when she flew away to be by the side of the Lord, Da said. He saw her rise like a candle flame, when I couldn't go near her any more.

Salvage

(After Tiepolo's *The Finding of Moses*:
Exodus 2: 4–9)

T he only other woman living in the hotel besides
Kate wasn't a guest, but the hotelier's girl-
friend, and she waited on him with quiet cere-
mony each night as he presided over the restaurant
from the corner of the dark inner room behind the bar.
A *pied-noir*, he'd come out to this corner of the colonies
with the first strangers' army a long time ago, and he
too had kept the flowery manners of the past, and a
formal mode of speech. She never sat down with him,
but now and then disappeared behind a curtain, where,
it was said, she also fixed pipes for him to smoke, later.
You could see from the ropes standing out on the backs
of his hands how the circulation of his blood had
slowed right down.

There were a few other women, younger than Kate,
who frequented the veranda of the hotel; they weren't
admitted into the dining room, or to the hotel's inner
courtyard. It was easy, once inside, to forget that a war
was going on, as a broad-leafed frangipani tree spread
scented shade on the tables set out underneath and
dropped waxy flowers on to the undiminished fine

57

linen of earlier days, while croissants were brought warm from the oven by the cook; he, too, had learned his trade from the former power. The other women were kept outside. They waited for customers at the *guéridons* on the veranda, with fizzy drinks from bottles with famous American brand names. You could tell from the cap, which was stamped off-register by hand, that they weren't the real thing.

Kate was shown the difference during the first days of her stay in the city, and she soon learned on her own account how everything was used more than once, passed from hand to hand, leaving a tiny doit of wealth behind as it went. Imitation wasn't really the word. Nor was fake, or cheat. It was more that things were adapted. Taken, named, made to resemble, to belong to a family of other things that offered them hospitality and added value. Salvaged.

She'd arrived in the final spasm of the counter-insurgents' offensive and she was to stay to within a few days of their success; she'd come because the man she'd recently married was reporting there for a London paper, and seeing the news of mounting catastrophe after he'd left had made her so frightened for his safety, she chose to join him. Passing the billboards made her imagine worse terrors than she would ever come across in reality – she was right in some ways. But it had been a risk, less on account of the danger the war presented than the nuisance she might become to him, as indeed it turned out. Her female presence undercut his heroic witness to the general savagery, the régime's reprisals, the horror of the rebels' attacks. Though the city would fall, it was at that time still the most protected fortress of the whole country, out of range of the rebel army's artillery, under strict curfew from dusk to dawn and seething with soldiers of the allied armies come to help save the incumbent government. She loved her husband much more than he requited, and because she was young and girlish with it, she felt that life had dealt her a hand with undue generosity. So she liked to provoke his cold impatience and prove her devotion by forgiving it and loving him the more.

One of the other journalists in the hotel played go-between on her behalf; after that, she befriended two of the bargirls, learned their first names, Solange and Noelle, and went to eat with them off formica and steel tables, bowls of spicy soup and dishes of fried fish after – sometimes, for it was the rainy season – plunging knee deep through the monsoon flood that swelled with tidal power in the streets every evening, to reach the place down some alley the girls knew was cheap and good. Kate paid, it was the least she could do. She would see Solange and Noelle separately, and she never sat with them on the veranda for fear of causing embarrassment: a soldier might think she was turning a trick as well, and as she was white, she offered unfair competition – though in her own country she was considered a young woman with pleasant features, but certainly no siren. Solange giggled when they walked along side by side, for Kate soon outstripped her and then had to stop to let her draw level again; Kate was wearing

cotton trousers and sandals in the heat, and her usual
gait was a stride, whereas Solange wore the country's
traditional costume, silk, tight-fitting, and she had tiny
beaded sandals with gilt high heels, so that she furled
and unfurled when she moved like the kite-tails that
streamed from some of the yards in the city where
children cut out relief agency ricebags and stitched
them to a frame of jetsam. This was another of their
reclamations, another secondary use, another salvage,
transforming the foreign into the native.

The journalist who had effected Kate's introduction
to Solange – it was necessary because she could have
been an official, a medical worker, a missionary, intent
on stopping her practise her trade – pointed out to her
that even the bras in vogue in the country had been
colonised: 'They're all uplift and points like the nose of
mortar shells – the style that went out at home with
hula hoops!'

When Kate went to the room where Solange lived,
she expected something like the brothels of Amster-
dam: a pallet spread with a white sheet, a bidet on a
stand, a towel, a mirror, a curtain, a calendar with a
photograph of a Swiss chalet or a Cotswold lane. She
travelled there alongside her in a different cyclo;
through the swirling putty water her wrinkled old
driver pedalled. The cyclo drivers were either too old
or too young to be conscripted, and as this meant a
pensioner or a child, Kate sat back helplessly pricked
by the sight of the man's chicken calves as she was
drawn through the muddy torrent and the hooting,

kerosene fog of traffic by someone for whom she'd give up her seat on the tube if she was at home. 'What else can you do?' Richard said to her when she moped about it. 'Don't be silly. They need the money, your hire puts bread on their plate, rice in their ricebowl. There are quite enough beggars round the place without your helping to create more by refusing to ride the cyclos. Come on.'

It turned out that Solange lived in a small wooden cabin on legs, polished and plain and flat-bottomed, like the cobles built for easy beaching Kate had known as a child on summer holidays in Yorkshire, but stranded here under a canopy of banana and some flowering trees, with her mother and two children, one who looked about five, the other a baby, an infant, but mute with the slate-blank eyes she knew from other children in the city streets. Solange showed her a photograph of the elder child's father, resorted to bargirl slang to describe their sweet and eternal love: 'You are my number one baby, my oochy poochy sweetiepie,' she chanted, quoting him. 'Solange, my honeypot, you're good enough to lick all over.' He was about twenty in the army snapshot, with a moustache, a white GI with an Italian name. He had been going to volunteer for a second tour; he'd promised to send money for Tony Junior, she was still waiting, still hoping, though it had clearly been years. Oh, it was so bloody typical, such utter stale buns, Kate could have slapped Solange. She had hoped that she was making it up, that she didn't know who the father was, she'd rather her life was a

racket, wanton anarchy, ferocious, cynical chaos, than
have her duped and asking for more. Yet wanting to
hit her, Kate saw, was the invitation her swaying sweet
baby-talking presence issued, the drowned kitten
seductiveness she'd learned.

Meanwhile, Solange's mother, in black pyjamas,
was squealing and flapping at the child until he went
outside again holding the baby and stopped gawping at
the roundeye woman with their mother. When had she
started work again after this infant? Kate saw a gash,
imagined tender walls, sore breasts, and firmly set such
thoughts aside.

'I no want im fight. Not like other kids,' said Solange. 'Soon he go to army, get killed.' She pointed at
the child who was now holding the baby in his arms.
'Junior eight years old now.' It was less hot in her hut
than outside, but her lip was pearled, and she wiped
her face with a towel, then handed the aluminium
waterpot to her mother to fill from the standpipe in the
street outside.

Kate was large for the room; she became aware of
her heft as she sat on the stool Solange indicated, and
waited while the pot began to rattle on the primus lit
on the step outside. The boy was now playing under
the eave of the hut's floor; looking for ants, for spiders.
He'd left the baby lying on the ground on a mat in the
shade of the wall. Solange said, 'She sleep now.'

The bed was in the corner; there was a curtain, a
picture, of a Filippino Lippi Madonna. Solange was
clearly better off than some of the other girls, who

worked the alleys and were firmly kept from even the veranda of the hotel. She still had her teeth, for one thing. 'The blowjob experts have them pulled,' one of the other guests in the hotel had informed her one night. 'When they're kids. The earlier the better. Soldiers don't like taking those kind of risks.'

At Solange's she was drinking tea from a cup with a dragon pattern on it like the set her parents had in Hebden Bridge; it was a different shape, however, more like an eggcup. She wondered what Solange did on the bed in the corner; she thought about her mother and the children in the room with her. She had seen families, all curled up together, kindle-like, using one another's legs and backs for pillows, sometimes out by the traffic on the pavement where it was cooler than under the tin roofs of the shanties. They could sleep through a lot; they had learned to sleep through the mortar explosions since the shelters had been flooded out and the attacks were gradually closing in, the centre of the city coming into range.

'You take him home with you, Kate. You call up Tony. Then Tony Junior go to college, go with you.'

'I live in England.'

'England, America, same, same. Yes? You rich. You take him when you go England. Him learn quick.'

Tony Junior had come in again, encumbered by the baby, who clung to him like a growth.

Kate nodded, but said, 'I can't, Solange. It isn't possible. I'm sorry.'

When she left, she gave her $20, two, three tricks'

worth, maybe more. The boy ran for a cyclo. Solange smoothed the note between her pale slender fingers and smiled. She tapped a tooth, gold, as was fashionable.

'I sell this, bribe officials, stop him go army.'

The city was full of business; though there were shortages, there was also surplus, and bartering was brisk on the pavements. Medicines beyond their due date lay on rush mats in neat piles like towers of toy bricks, beside varied anatomies of hardware and dead soldiers' paraphernalia – contraband watches, radios, hi-fis, compasses, electrical parts and bicycle parts, recharged batteries, boots, coats, wallets, belts – as well as rebottled Dewar's and Black Label and Jim Crow and Kentucky sour mash with the wrong screw-tops. Their minders were mostly children, boys. With small, lithe hands, the vendors would clutch at her arm, and screech at her, begging her to buy. If she didn't want anything from their display of wares, they had plenty more stuff elsewhere they could fetch, they had anything she might want. This was the world of the jokes she overheard, 'You want my little sister? No? You want my little brother? You want nice big smack – cheap, cheap? You like sucky sucky?'

Girl children were not so visible; they were indoors, she supposed, under protection or already conducting curtained business of their own. In the market, the slimy, fetid, sprawling downtown market in the Chinese quarter of the city, there was still plenty of food for sale, much strangling of various fowl and gutting of fish, crabs lumbering in wicker cages and jackfruit splitting at the seams and ripely adding to the mixed perfumes in the contrived darkness. The first time Kate went, she was attracted by the toys, the heaps of paper boats and houses, horses and mobiles, figures of men and women made of indigo- and cochineal-dyed rice paper stitched by hand. She bought a rider on a stiff-legged steed, a pagoda, and a bundle of paper money in brilliant scarlet with gold-leaf stamps on it, while the market women roared with laughter at her, calling out names. Later she was told, 'They were shouting "Peasant" – because of your hat.' (She had taken to wearing a tribal straw hat against the sun.) She also learned, from another informant, that her toys were funerary offerings: 'The gooks burn them on the pyre, so that the dead can take that stuff to heaven with them. It's symbolism, far-out Booudhist symbolism.' Kate took them up to her hotel room, still loyal to their delicate craft, though she realised they wouldn't travel well.

Solange's boy was the first child Kate was offered. There were no babies arranged on the rush mats and no booths at the market which dangled them for sale. But as goods, babies came her way, along with other things she could have tried if she had a fancy to. She was never offered a girl baby, however. Her own singular state remained intact, if anything became deeper. When she commented to Richard, after the third child she was asked to take, that she was surprised they were all boys, he said, 'It stands to reason. They don't want them to be called up. It's a good story. I should write it. But it's Human Interest, and they want War Games – the Allied Strategy, the Body Count, the Weapon Stockpile, the odds on a ceasefire, etc. Why don't you do it? It'd keep you busy.'

'I've never written an article,' she said.

'You write law reports, you brief barristers. You know how to string your thoughts together on paper.'

She began to listen in on the talk in the hotel.

'Where can you get contraception in the city?' she asked.

One of the wire men answered, after a mock display of shock, 'Anywhere and everywhere. They're free at the PX; they're in every bar that's got a john, and the girls have got them on them.'

'So why's the birth rate so high?'

Then she met Jinty, and found comfort in the company of another woman. Jinty was short and plump and solid like a riding mistress; her hair clasped her head closely as if used to a hard hat. She came from Surrey, and lived in Cobham when she was at home, among gorse bushes and pines. But she specialised in children in crisis, famine relief, and the administration of foreign aid. The charity organisation called Sangrail had sent her to this war, to see if there was any way through the political deadlock; the charities' money to the government was routinely siphoned off, money to the rebels was against UN rules; the counter-insurgents were holed up in villages badly needing supplies of all kinds, but officially they did not exist, so it was not possible even to put into gear any means of helping civilians in the territory they held. After a month of impasse with officials, when Kate met her at a function in the Canadian envoy's villa Jinty was concentrating her attention on the city's orphanages. 'I'm practical,' she told her. 'Wrangling with colonels isn't my cup of tea at all. I don't want to waste time wittering, though the Lord knows I still have to do a heck of a lot of it.'

The next day, Kate went with her to a children's hospital, down the sidestreets heavy with kerosene and churning with cyclos, to the old European quarter of the city, where three Belgian nuns in a convent founded in the last century were nursing foundlings, some of whom had been left on their doorstep, while others had been brought in from the war, from burned villages, from the evacuated rebel-held countryside.

'It doesn't interest me, who wins,' Jinty was saying. 'Does it you? No? Good. Let the generals argue the toss with one another. There's plenty to be done while they chinwag.'

They were at the door of the infirmary. In Italy, at the Innocenti hospital in one of the northern towns, Kate had once seen the special compartment in the door, where the babies used to be put. It was like a night safe in a bank's outer wall – the packet was passed through without one party seeing the other. But here there was no sign of the place's purpose, of the bundled children delivered to the step, as she had half expected. The nun who came to open the door to them wasn't a foreigner, but a native, wearing a grey veil and pearl-headed pins to secure it to the white wimple that covered her ears and neck. She kissed Jinty, and left one hand on her shoulder with lingering tenderness; they exchanged words in French, and Kate recognised in the missionary's voice the West African accent of fellow students from her days at Gray's Inn.

'Soeur Philippe,' the nun introduced herself. The skin of her palm was dry and hard. 'Come and see our children.' She had that way of smiling nuns catch from statues: beatific, and without a trace of laughter.

This first infirmary gave model treatment, compared to other establishments Kate was to visit. At first she thought she was doing as Richard said, and gathering material for an article on the plight of the abandoned children and orphans of the war, but soon she found that without consciously embarking on helping Jinty, she was running errands and carrying out certain tasks for her. There was, as Jinty had said, plenty to do. In the Belgian nuns' hospital the children lay two to a cot, one at each end, on a sheet, with a nappy on and a bottle each tied to a strut in the cot's side near their mouth; most of them were far too weak to reach the teat even if they were developed enough to roll or otherwise make a move towards it. So someone had to go round and try to fit the babies' mouths to their feed and stimulate them to suck. There wasn't time to pick a child up and nurse him – or her – individually; there were far too many in need. Starvation had turned their clocks back; they looked like medical photographs of gestating embryos, with huge frontal lobes and tiny sperm-like limbs. She could have scooped one of them into the palms of her hands like a frog.

'You see, they are frequently born premature. The mothers are not eating enough, in their bodies they are – how shall I say – not healthy . . . Their way of life . . .' Soeur Philippe joined her hands over her habit as if praying. 'They do not leave their children to die. No, they abandon them so that they have a chance to survive. Somewhere else. Here, or, if possible, in Europe, America. They dream . . . but, you know . . .' She put out her hand and touched a baby's face; the open eyes, huge as an owl's, did not flicker. 'On fait de son mieux.'

Jinty was examining the register: 'I need to make a copy of the figures, to send to London. We must have facts. It's not to be believed otherwise.'

The nun shook her head. 'The register is out of date, it is hard to keep it up. We pray at the burials, of course, we remember all of them in our prayers. But the record – we don't have time for the record.' Jinty handed Kate the book, where in theory each child was to be entered – case history, weight, race, symptoms, treatment, outcome (discharge to another orphanage, or death). 'Make a few copies anyway – and come back.'

Kate took the ledger; she tried various shops with photocopiers, but none was working – contraband toner was harder to fake than bourbon and Coke – so eventually she went round to the daily briefing centre and used the journalists' office facilities, thinking how stupid she was not to have thought of that immediately. She was confused, the children had confused her, they made her feel lewd in her healthiness and her strength. The smell of them was still in her nostrils, the leaky milk-and-piss sickliness of their feeble hold on life.

That night in the hotel she spoke up, from the table where she was sitting on her own – Richard had again gone up-country with a general to write up the regime's supposed progress – and she addressed the room, over the head of the Agence France Presse rep who was also dining on his own, directing her comments to the group of wire service journalists and other papers' stringers who were eating together. 'I saw about two hundred babies today,' she began. 'They've been abandoned in the last few months, since the offensive started. Most of them looked as if they were dying. They're mostly half black and half white. The mothers are all bargirls, apparently.'

'Yeah,' said one newspaperman. 'The whole fucking country's one big brothel. That's our present to the people: we teach the women how to fuck. That's freedom. That's a law of the free market.'

'Who's going to use a rubber when his life is on the line? It's tough.' This was another man, joining the conversation. 'Those guys, they want to leave something of themselves behind.' The veteran newspaperman, famous for hard-hitting coverage, spread his hands and shrugged.

Another put in, 'Two hundred? That's a lot of children. I reckon they're telling us something about what's happening out there. Nobody wants to get caught with anything incriminating on them when the end comes, now do they? And what would be more incriminating than a little roundeye babba with funny-coloured skin?'

The most famous reporter of all nodded at Kate and called out, 'It's like we wrote at the start of the war, it's still the same story. "You gotta destroy the village in order to save it." You gotta leave your fucking child if you want him to stay alive. The only safe place to be is elsewhere.'

The next day, Kate joined Jinty in a different orphanage, this one for babies and children who could feed themselves and obey their minder's order to sit in line on potties and perform. Many of these did not have foreign fathers, but had lost their parents, either through death during a raid or through dispersal, as they took flight from a village under attack or were scattered as they stole into the city at night for safety. The authorities in this establishment were secular, and local: The Good Fortune and Long Life Prudential Society.

'You should watch out,' one reporter said when she'd finished telling them. 'They'll bleed you for all you're worth, that little lot. It's Madam So-and-so's outfit, isn't it? Her good works, my ass. It's just a cover for far more important business. She's using it to launder – you take a little look at the books, little lady, and you see if you can make head or tail of the finances of the Good Fortune and Long Life Prudential Society – if they've got any books they'll let you see.'

When she brought it up with Jinty, the older woman replied, 'Journalists like plots. I'm not interested in plots, and the people aren't characters to me, they're not pieces on some almighty chessboard. Close your mind to them. If you think about who you're helping you'll never do a thing. There'll always be a good reason to sit on your bottom and do nothing.'

That day they went to a city shelter for disabled children. These were orphans of all ages, and their handicaps were in some cases the results of wounds – bombs, shrapnel, gas – but in other cases congenital or the result of neglect, of malnutrition. When Kate arrived in the former warehouse, the reek of disinfectant was overwhelming. It was dark inside, and though this at least helped keep down the temperature under the metal roof, the lack of windows made the atmosphere inside asphyxiating. First she noticed that the walls were dripping and the dirt floor was covered in a film of water tinged with the blue-grey bubbles of some toilet cleansing fluid; then she saw that the children were soaking too, lying nappy-less on rubber sheets draped on iron bedsteads or on the floor, where ammoniac puddles had also collected.

'They hose them down in the morning,' Jinty told her. 'It's the quickest way to clean up the ones who are incontinent, and restore some level of hygiene to the room.' She looked round the room, as Kate swallowed, and went on, 'Boys and girls are all mixed in together, so we can't vouch for another sort of hygiene.'

Jinty had commandeered a team of allied soldiers to plumb in showers and basins, linked to the standpipe in the street outside; Kate had accompanied her to the army depot and watched her rustling up the equipment, the parts and the fittings, from the sergeant on duty. They began moving the children from one side of their dark quarters to the other, to separate the boys from the girls. To the ones with power in their arms, Kate gave piggy-backs; their heads on her shoulders like stones, their breath distempered by starvation. One girl patted her hair, and said something softly, twisting her head around to smile in her eyes. She was admiring it, Kate realised, admiring it for its difference from her own, in lightness of colour and fluffiness of texture.

She helped put up a partition, to give some privacy to the older girls who had started to menstruate. It was built of tough cartons that had delivered something marked Fragile to the assisting army; they'd been salvaged from one of the many public dumps before someone else could take them to turn them into a whole family's shelter. Jinty, with a male army nurse she had also commandeered, was washing some of the children and covering them in clothing they had brought. On examination close up, many of their bodies were terribly damaged, but there were no dressings available, and only bleach for disinfectant. A softish, wadded parcel from England had miraculously passed through the thieving hands of customs and other authorities; it proved to be full of teddy bears.

Trying to tend the children, Kate was reminded of the heaps of rubbish behind the foreigners' haunts, and near other places of abundance, like the market, where the natives swarmed to pick over the fruit and vegetables, the burst packaging, the rags and débris. The little boy lying prone on the rubber sheeting whom she began swabbing looked as if he had fallen from a tree on to stones where wasps and worms had feasted on the tears in his flesh. She clenched her teeth to stop herself gagging, her repugnance increased by shame that she should feel disgust at all.

Jinty noticed, and told her, kindly, 'Listen, old girl, no need to linger. You need time to get used to this sort of thing. Go on, have a breath of fresh air outside. If you can find some.'

Richard came back from his expedition to the counter-insurgents' territory. He was frustrated in his attempts to file, because the government censors had picked up his denunciations of the three-cornered civil war; he was furious. In the hotel, the number of pressmen had grown; from the corner of the dining room where he was waited on by his companion, the proprietor now rewrote the hotel charges on a nightly basis as prices rose; the wines drunk improved in labels and vintage as he dug deeper into the last of the cellar. There was a trade in passports and visas at the bar; in other things as well. Contractors arrived and were busy; the beggars at the hotel door grew bolder, as did the rats, sometimes making an appearance before the dining room was empty to snatch at fallen scraps. The embassies notified their nationals to leave. 'You're to get out, Kate, there's no two ways about it,' said Richard. 'It's the end, and I've got to stay as long as I can. But you . . .'

She tried to make love to him that night. She saw the children's bodies in her mind's eye, their gaze shadowless, like the moon in eclipse. She wanted the sap and the kick of sex to move this darkness and lift the heavy bodies of the orphans where they were lodged in her, torpid and undigested. But Richard wouldn't, he too lay leaden, a reproach to her, as if he were saying in his unresponsiveness, How could you at a time like this? She was half thinking to herself, We should have a child ourselves, a strapping, crowing, pink-and-white child who knows how to express hunger and discomfort and ask for everything, not like these inert lumps of flesh in their silence and their stink. All the time she'd been with Jinty trying to help her with the orphans she'd never shed a tear. It had left her as numb and cold as if she were made of ten-day-old suet, and she hated herself for it and for not being able to get through to Richard: he was out there on the front line, fighting, even when he was in bed with her, and women had no place there, no, nor love either. So she wept now for herself, lying naked in the stifling room, hearing the distant boom and crackle of the mortars and the scritch of the rats in the walls.

The Mermaids in the Basement

I watch the big English who come one day see my mother
drink tea with her I follow her offer her cigarettes the man
gave me sell sell. She say no cigarettes but she give me two
quarters an tell me no smoke myself have something eat she
no recognise me I go with her she go to sisters' infirmary
where they take babies she ask why you follow me I tell her
you pretty woman you kind woman she laugh she say go
away home I say please I come see you again tomorrow she
say no no I say please again she gets angry shoo shoo little
boy I no have more money I say please she no say name of
hotel but I know where she stay (she no realise I know) but
she say tomorrow she come one more time say goodbye she
leaving she sad this country number one people in it so sweet
and never complain she say. I find my mother home she sick
now an I tell her and she say, Take Theresa so I take my
sister mother give us money for cyclo, I only ride cyclo one
time before and I tell driver go sisters' infirmary, he go and I
leave Theresa in basket with blanket and other things on the
step

 first nobody come and I hidin by door nearby an waitin an
watchin hopin big English come like she say an then I see her
she hot she puff she stop an make little cry when she see
basket and baby then she pick up Theresa and hug Theresa
an look in basket I wait see what she do then if she ring bell
give Theresa to door sister she do she go in with sister they
talk talk high voices big English I hear she cry again

 my mother burn many offering she light candle though she
sick she walk to church to make special prayer for Theresa
The big English no want to take me I too grownup take care

76

*of things here now so mother pray she take Theresa and we
all be leaving soon soon for to find Tony*

After the fall of the city later that year, and the establishment of the new régime, Kate returned there to
join Jinty, who had remained throughout, and to complete the adoption process of the child she had finally
chosen when she found her lying on the steps of the
Belgian nuns' infirmary on her last day in the city,
just before she left because Richard – and the British
government representatives too, to be fair to him –
insisted that she did. Jinty helped her with the paper-
work; by the end, she'd spent some £10,000, she
reckoned, acquiring her daughter. But it was a small
price to pay for Theresa, of course. That was her given
name: it was written on a paper and plastic bracelet
which must have been borrowed from a hospital and
left in the basket, alongside one or two other tokens.
Just like a fairytale, and the child did feel to her like a
fairy boon, she had to admit. Theresa, who had lain
there in her way as if predestined, who had put her
arms around her neck confidingly when she picked her
up that first time as if she knew her and understood
that she could care for her, that she would care for her.
She had turned over inside at her touch: Theresa was
like the spark in flint and she lit Kate back to life.

Jinty said, 'A lot of people bleat about uprooting
children from their culture and whatever. Culture?
When you haven't got enough to eat? When you'll be
on the streets by the age of ten? Oh, they're dear, clever

little things, and they might manage to survive, but what kind of a life will it be? Don't let the doubters and the purists torment you, you go ahead, Kate, give Theresa an English life, give her pony clubs, ballet classes, meat and two veg, Beefeaters, the battle of Trafalgar, the lot. Hell's bells, one has to believe in something. Besides, she's half-and-half anyway – her father could have been God knows what.'

When Theresa was six and began going to school all day, Kate took on full-time work for Sangrail as an expert on refugees, specialising in adoption and immigration law. Richard was usually travelling, still avoiding the conjunction of marriage, still covering the hot spots (but for another paper now – his old one had been taken over and now, in the interest of profits, used only news agencies' reports). So Kate decided she couldn't manage with only part-time help any longer, and began to employ a housekeeper. She picked her first from the large population of boat people whom she was helping to get the right papers for the country of their eventual choice; Kate knew her way through the red tape – refugee law, immigration law, political asylum – and how to finger exactly the right subsection of the right bill for her client. Canada was very popular, and so were some of the Caribbean countries. It became her special field of expertise, and a trickle of women from Theresa's birthplace – and sometimes their husbands – had passed through her house and lived for a time in the basement flat. It wasn't an ideal relationship, of course. She would have preferred not to be an employer at all, a 'mistress', a 'madam'.

Kate sometimes thought of Solange and Noelle and wondered what had happened to them; how badly they had been punished for fraternisation, how well they had survived the new régime's 'lustration' programmes. She once or twice asked her contacts for news, but it was very difficult to trace someone when all you knew about her was that she had been a bargirl with a child or two, information which would not be the most helpful way to identify her, given the character of the new government.

One day a refugee liaison centre Kate worked with telephoned her about a case: an economics exchange student in Paris had applied for his mother to leave and join him. She wanted to work in England, she had a little English. He was making approaches to transfer his scholarship to LSE, in order to continue his studies. He was bright, and he was resolved, at present, to return to his country; he had prospects and he was not seeking residency or citizenship for himself. As for his mother, he had specifically given them Kate's name as a possible sponsor. Would she take up the case?

Madame Ng's first name was Phong; she arrived to start her post as housekeeper in the summer holidays of Theresa's eleventh year (or what was thought to be her eleventh year, on the basis of a conjectured age of three months when she was found). Kate interviewed her beforehand; she asked her how she and her son had known about her. Phong smiled: she had heard about

Kate in the city, everyone had. Kate was straining to catch something that seemed familiar in Phong's face, something that sounded familiar in her voice, but every time she thought she caught a flicker, it passed. It was like trying to remember a name; it's on the tip of your tongue but it just won't form itself. She dismissed the fleeting resemblance as fantasy, stirred up by a yearning for reparation, a sense of loss, of the page irrevocably turned. Kate thought then that she might never be able to stop feeling this . . . interconnectedness with the women in the city who had lived those lives and had the babies – it wasn't guilt, exactly, but something shared, as if when she was holding Theresa she wanted to turn into one of them and look in the mirror and find herself changed to match her daughter.

Phong looked so much older than Solange would have been, with her hair cut short and straight and her torso slightly bent – an abdominal operation had left a lumpy scar, so she listed forward when she walked as if to shield her vulnerable tissue from bumps and angles. Kate sometimes found herself scanning her, wondering about Theresa's real mother, and her imagination would begin to whirr and she'd have to tell herself to stop it, stop it. That way madness lies: a hall of mirrors and no end to the reflections.

Phong was very proud of her son, quite rightly; and the new régime's debriefing about America had impressed her deeply. She didn't want to emigrate there, unlike some of her predecessors, but to stay in London and work for Kate. That was what she said, what she insisted she wanted. It was hard to get work papers for her, but Kate promised to do her best (though she also pointed out to her that housekeeper/ nanny wasn't the best-paid job in the world, especially at the wages Kate could afford, nor the most rewarding in other ways).

Theresa soon outstripped her new nanny in height – in spite of her puny size in the first year of life, she'd since been nourished on muesli and kiwi and other vitamin-rich foodstuffs and had grown rangy in limb, with a light sheen on her skin like a hazelnut. Moving with the quicksilver energy of childhood, she tended to be impatient with her refugee minders, especially with their lack of English and their timorous ways of negotiating London transport systems, and Kate would have to scold her and teach her to make allowances for newcomers. But from the start Phong seemed to dust off the little girl's prickliness. 'I love Mummy best, this much,' Theresa would say, stretching her arms wide. 'Then Daddy, this much' – bringing them in a little – 'And then you, Phong, this much!' She'd then stretch them out again, hooting. One time, playing this game, her mouth was full of spring rolls Phong had cooked for her, and Kate stood in the doorway, watching her at the kitchen table as Phong dished up another. 'You eat now, Theresa, and don't chit-chat so much,' responded Phong, already busy scouring the pan at the sink.

Kate felt a tweak of jealousy, but she squashed it. It would be stupid to mind that Theresa at last had a

81

nanny she really seemed to like. She had always wanted her to feel something in common with the people she came from. And after all, it was the dream of every working mother to find someone who could stand in for her, when she couldn't be there all the time to take care of her child herself.

II

HUSBANDS & LOVERS

The First Time

The serpent had decided to diversify; the market economy demanded it. Jeans, soft drinks, bicycles and sunglasses had learned to present themselves in subtly different guises; so could he.

He took a training course in nutrition. In his first job (for he showed talent), he was issued with an instantly printed label identifying him as 'Lola – Trainee Customer Service Assistant', and he wangled himself a pitch on the Tropical Fruit stand in the Tropical Fruit promotion that was taking place in order to add a little cheer to the London winter.

To attract the customers' attention, the serpent now known as Lola was togged up in tropical splendour and he put on his deepest and brownest syrupy voice to match. There were OAPs with plastic shopping bags on wheels and hair in their noses; they tasted the little cubes of fragrant juicy this and that which Lola had cut up and flagged with their proper name and country of origin, but one said he would think about it, dear, and another made a face and said the stringy bits were too stringy. Lola wasn't sure the game was worth the candle in their case. She was after brighter prizes. The serpent in her liked fresh material; he hoped for a challenge. (Though pity, it would turn out after all, wasn't unknown to him.)

Then Lola spotted a candidate: a likely lass, a young one made just as she fancied, quite ready for pleasure, pleasure of every sort, a hard green bright slip of a girl, barely planted but taking root, and so she held out in her direction a nifty transparent plastic cup like a nurse's for measuring out dosages in hospital, with one of the tasty morsels toothpicked and labelled inside it, and urged her to eat. (She was speaking aloud in the new soft brown demerara voice, but under her breath she was cooing and hissing in another voice altogether which she hoped her young shopper would listen to, secretly. This was a trick the serpent had perfected over centuries of practice.)

'Come here, my little girly, I have just the thing for a cold day, bring some sunshine back into your life.

> (I know what it's like, it's written all over you.
> He fucked you to death three days ago – oh, is it
> a whole week? – and you haven't heard from him
> since. Your face is pale, your brow is wan and
> you can't understand what you did wrong. Well,
> you can tell me all about it)

'There's nothing Lola your Trainee Customer Service Assistant can't provide. It's Tropical Fruit week – just move over this way – we have passion fruit and pawpaw (that's papaya by another name) and prickly pear and pitahaya and guava and tamarillo and

phylaris and grenadilla. Not to mention passion fruit.
Each one has been flown here from the lands of milk
and honey where they grow naturally, as in the original
garden of paradise, and they're full of just that milk
and honey, I'm telling you, you can hear the palm
trees bending in the breeze on the beach and the surf
breaking in creamy froth on the sand and they reach
the parts other things don't reach

> (the tingly bits, the melting bits and rushes-to-
> the head and the rushes to places elsewhere than
> the head – well I shan't go on, but your troubles
> are at an end if you just come a little bit closer,
> so I can pick up the signals in your dear little
> fluttering heart, my sweet, and whisper in your
> ear)

'As I say, it's Tropical Fruit week and this is the
Tropical Fruit stand! With a dozen different varieties of
fruit from all over the world, many new, exciting and
delicious flavours for you to sample, and

> (let me add this under my breath so only you can
> hear – they all have different powers they can
> work wonders in all kinds of different ways –
> they're guaranteed to fix up your little problems
> before you can snap your fingers and say What
> the hell, and what the hell, I know all about that,
> I know the hell you're in, believe me.
>   And I also know – I do – how to stop it
> hurting, my dear little one)

'I should know, because I'm fresh from the Healthy Eating consultancy course in our company head-quarters in Stanton St James, Gloucestershire. We were given an intensive fortnight of nutritional experience, and so there's nothing I can't tell you now about fruit –'

And the serpent, to his great joy, saw that the young girl was getting interested and coming closer, with her shopping list crumpled under one hand on the bar of the supermarket trolley and the other twiddling a strand of her hair near her chin, as she drew near to look at Lola's spread of little plastic cups with pieces of fruit in each one, so close that Lola could hear her thinking,

i was all clenched up cos i was scared it's not every-day i do it you know in fact i don't do it very often though looking at me you might think so and i like to make out i'm a one cos otherwise you look a bit of a wimp don't you i mean everyone else is doing it, aren't they? and my mother said keep smiling the men don't like scenes they don't like glooms if you want to drive a man away just keep that down at the mouth look on your face and the wind'll change men don't like a woman all down in the dumps who'd want to spend a minute with you it'd be like passing the time of day with a ghoul

And Lola took charge of the situation, it was her job to bring a little sunshine back into winter; pleasure was her speciality. So she began,

'Take mango for instance, now the instructions say,

88

"Make sure the rind is rosy-yellow and slightly yielding to the touch – green mangoes are inedible." Just
like it says there, on the label, a mango, when it's
properly ripe and ready, is full and juicy and its sweetness runs all over your hands and gives off this deep
rich scent –'

> (I don't have to go on, do I? A good man is going
> to know that and if he don't know it, he's no
> good and you can drop him, my sweet, and find
> another one who understands these things. The
> first point you must get into your little head,
> sweetheart, is that if you were clenched up like
> you said it wasn't anybody's fault but his –)

i tried to be lighthearted and cheerful while it was
going on but it kept getting to me all the same and
making me sad, sex does that to you it lifts you up but
it doesn't last it drops you down again from a great
height and now i can't concentrate on anything cos i
keep seeing him doing things to me and me doing them
back i was trying to keep a brave face on it but i know i
was disappointing not passionate like he knows it from
other girls it wasn't new to him like it was to me he
knows that   i could sense it but i don't like the neigh-
bours to hear anything cos when they're at it and i hear
and mum is out and i'm alone it makes me feel funny
Lola carries on, talking over the girl's thoughts,
which are coming across to her loud and clear. 'Take
this guava for instance,' she tells her. 'It's in perfect
condition. Sometimes when you pierce one of these

fruits, they're not quite ripe yet. You have to wait for
the ones that aren't ready, you can't rush them. But the
ones that are overripe, gone soft and spongy, you have
to throw those away . . .'

(don't you worry any more, my little girly,
you'll be fine. You're just lacking confidence,
that's all it is, and you wanted to please him,
when really you should just think how much
pleasure there's in it for you. Never forget that,
it's the first rule. My sweet little girly, you're a
perfect little girly and he's a fool if I know men –
and I do – forget him and find another one who'll
appreciate you)

it's a bit shocking, really, i didn't expect such a mess,
both of us leaking this and that, i did melt at first,
stickiness afterwards he seemed to like it, he held on to
me tight, he asked me if i cared for him and i said i
did, and his heart was thumping and it seemed like a
promise it was a promise, it must have been some kind
of a promise . . . but then nothing not another sight of
him not a word what did i do wrong what can i do
now

(when he comes back and he will you know he'll
be round with his tongue hanging out you must
be ready so come closer still – you are a sweet
and tender pretty little girl, aren't you, yum
yum, no wonder he liked you he's probably just
frightened of coming back because your hold on

him's too strong believe me, I know. You're at
just that dangerous age, and your hair smells
good, vanilla and grass and peach and a trace of
sweat, that's good, very good –)

The young girl's head was very near Lola now, as
she bent over the little measuring cups with their pink
and yellow and crimson offerings, sniffing at this one
and that one, daring, daring to taste one.

'Peaches don't count as Tropical but they have res-
torative powers too, I'm telling you, and now we can
grow them all the year round, that's the wonder of
modern agronomy – agronomy – the science of growing foods

(anyhow, darling, just any one of these Tropical
Fruits will give him what he wants from you
and then you'll have him in the palm of your
hand. Try slipping him a fat cactus fruit, with
the spines cut off, mind – or if you're ambitious,
try pawpaw – papaya by another name as I was
saying and it's no accident that this is papa-fare,
ha ha. It's a fruit for daddy's girls, firm and
slippery, yes!)

'and its juice makes an excellent meat tenderiser if
you want to add it to a marinade or you can just open it
and eat it all, yes, seeds and all – Or there's tamarillo
here, it's full of rich pulp under the tight shiny skin and
the flavour's sweet and sour when it's ripe, and has
many culinary uses, in desserts as well as savoury

dishes . . . Eat it when the skin's turned a deep red, and the fruit's firm but yielding to gentle pressure . . .'

(that's right, you start giggling, you'll be fine even if it's all over with him there'll soon be another one – I'm telling you, live for passion there's nothing better and that's the second rule and all men and women are fools who don't grasp it)

it began like that he said, Trust me, and then you open up first your mouth and his mouth and then, well . . . sometimes i envy men, they know what other women are like, i wonder if i'm like the other ones, he must have had lots he felt like he knew what he was doing. i was a bit scared, he's older than me just two years but it makes a difference and he's got a reputation at school that's what made me interested in the first place so i bit down on my fears, other girls do it all the time i must get on with mum's shopping it might give that assistant ideas, my hanging around here maybe i should try one of her fruits she looks silly standing there in that tropical outfit with the headcloth and the fruit earrings dangling and the bangles over her surgical gloves she's using a little sharp knife with these funny knobbly and lumpy fruits she's egging on to customers, the OAPs with their shopping bags on wheels and their nose hair sprouting, so now it's my turn and i point to one of the little plastic cups with the fruit inside on a toothpick and she's saying to me,

'Go on try, you're under no obligation to purchase –

I don't even have the fruits here on my stand, you have
to go to the fruit and veg. section and choose your
own. We're here to educate the public, to raise the
standards of nutrition and health in the households of
this country, especially where there are children and
young people, growing up

> (like you, my dear, so silky and soft and lovely
> with just that whiff of unwashed . . .)

'There's pitahaya for you too – firm as a pear and
slightly perfumed, like rose petals – it's refreshing!
Here, you can eat it like a dessert fruit, you peel it
like this, lengthways, the rind comes off smoothly, it's
related to the prickly pear but this one hasn't got any
prickles. Or you can slice it into salads – add a dash of
colour to your salad bowl, keep the winter at bay with
Tropical Fruit from the parts of the world where frost
can't reach and the sun always shines, scoop out the
pink flesh and taste the sunshine!'

we didn't use anything it seemed mean to ask him to
as if i thought he was diseased or something so now i
don't know i could be pregnant – are you happy to be
pregnant? the ads ask – i could be i suppose – i can feel
something inside me it's like a letter y it's either a
sperm wriggling or it's one of those cells they go on
about on the telly reproducing itself all wrong and
giving me aids

> (now that was silly very silly you can't have the
> pleasure that's due to you, my girl, if you're

careless, that's the third rule. But if you bend
your ear I'll let you in on the way to have fun –
never do that again, this time you'll be all right, I
can tell, I can see and hear things other people
can't and)

'There's nothing like fresh fruit to build up your
immune system, clean out your insides, keep you
healthy and lean and full of energy . . .

(as I say, you're in luck this time but don't try
anything like that again)

'. . . in these days of pollution and other problems – I
mean we've all wised up to the devastation of the rain
forests and their connection to . . . well, I shan't talk
about meat-eating because we still have a butcher's
counter here – all free range, of course – but anyway
what with acid rain and the hole in the ozone layer and
the thinning of the oxygen supply and the little creepy-
crawly things out of the tap in your water – you need
Fruit! Fresh fruit, goes straight to the immune system
and kick-starts it into a new life . . .'

Eventually, the serpent was successful: his fresh,
young, sad target dropped her mother's shopping list
somewhere on the floor of the supermarket and forgot
everything that was on it and came home instead with

    1 mango
    1 pitahaya
    2 pawpaws

4 guavas
2 tamarillos
6 passion fruit
   and 13p change

Her mother said, 'Where's the shopping I asked you to get?' And so her daughter told her about Lola, about the Tropical Fruit stand and Tropical Fruit week. She kept quiet, however, about some of the other matters that had passed between her and the sales assistant.

Her mother scolded, her mother railed: 'In my day, an apple a day kept the doctor away – now you have to have –' she picked up the guavas and the soft but firm mango and the tubular and prickle-free pitahaya and smooth and slippery pawpaw – 'What do you do with this stuff anyway?'

'I've brought the leaflet – look!'

'Apples were good enough for us, and they should be good enough for you. And when I write down a pound of apples on the shopping list I mean a pound of apples, I don't mean any of this fancy rubbish. Your generation doesn't understand the meaning of no – you just believe in self, self, self, you want more, more, more. You think only of your own pleasure. You'll be the ruin of me. I don't know, I try to bring you up right . . .'

'Plump and rounded or long and thin, it has a distinctive firmness of texture and delicacy of aroma . . .' her daughter began, reading from the recipe leaflet provided, and she thought she heard her mother stifle a

snort as she kept on with the Tropical Fruit week promotion package.

if he doesn't come back that lady was right i'll just
find another one what she said made sense he thought
he was something but was he anything to write home
about anyhow i feel better about it already i'll go back
to school and i'll just make out it meant nothing to me
nothing and i don't care about him she was wicked she
was strong i liked her

Lola was still at the stand, back in the shop, doing
her patter, to other customers passing by:

'Guava, passion fruit, tamarillo! Let me just tell you
exactly how you can put each one to good use –'

And meanwhile she was thinking,

> (my little girly, you're young, you're
> inexperienced, but you'll soon know so much.
> You'll look back on this and you'll laugh or you
> won't even remember that you ever felt so pale
> and wan. In fact you might even look back and
> wish that you could feel something as sweet and
> real and true as this first-time pain you were
> feeling till I taught you the three principles of
> pleasure and set you on my famous primrose path)

Her mother took the leaflet out of her hand and
scanned it impatiently; she read:

> For a happy and healthy life!
> Take fresh fruit in season.
> Squeeze.

Ariadne after Naxos

(Ovid, *Metamorphoses*, Bk. VIII)

I was left here on the island at the height of the summer, and I decided to stay. It's October now, and the grapes on the terrace where Chloe and I eat our breakfast have turned purple. We can reach up into the vine and snap off the heavy bunches. It's an image of paradise; paradise was just such a garden as we enjoy here. Yet our fingers print gleaming lobes on the white bloom of the fruit's skin, and if the grapes fall to the tiled floor they leave Tyrian-dark stains that no amount of scouring will take away. You can't touch anything, even here in our sanctuary, without bringing about some change, and every contact carries us forward and on. Whereas I, for one, should like stasis, heavenly stasis.

Our terrace overlooks the convent's extensive lands: stepped terraces, tilted sunwards, of vegetables and herbs and fruits climb evenly towards the mountains in the distance; the house itself, a tawny stucco that blazes apricot in the sun glare, is veiled with flowering creepers. Now, in autumn, the dried calyxes hang on the braided stems among bright berries and juicy hips, seedpods as cunning as embroidered needlecases, spore-sacks like jewel boxes. Everywhere we walk there are new scents, and they keep a daily rhythm, exhaling different perfumes at dawn, at noon, at twilight. The blue-white mountain mass at the spine of the island guards our enclave to the north; the rose-coloured beach encloses us on the other. Every window in the convent luminously frames a section of the view, with the selective eye of a master painter. Now and then an earthquake tremor shakes us, for our island lies in a volcanic archipelago; then our fertile earth hisses through narrow fissures. Puffs of steam, smelling sulphurous and coloured pink and yellow like distress flares, erupt with sudden sharp sighs from the ground under our footsteps. I have to remember then that this place isn't a retreat to lull me, but a discipline to keep my senses alive and my faculties alert.

We have difficulty keeping this paradise in order: the earth outruns our efforts at husbandry. In the lemon grove below the main living quarters the trees are bowed with more fruit than we can ever squeeze or dry. We train the laden branches on a cradle of willow wands, but the lemons lie in the red irrigation runnels beneath, shrunken and browning. By the barn where we store apples the hives drip with honey. We can't keep pace with the bees. In the herb plot, the basil bed has become a field, the plants have grown leaves as big as lime trees' in a colder climate.

So much fruitfulness: like a wave, its greatest expansion is also its breaking point, when the fruit will lose

the shape that gives it its identity, its integrity. The
vegetables run to seed here; the bees will leave if we
can't clean out their combs for them and prepare them
new hives; the persimmon crop will rot. In the library,
the mice are busy making nests in the books. I empty
the traps each morning, but at night I hear more scam-
per in the rafters. But we can manage to keep a check
on excess; we can at least prevent complete encroach-
ment.

We're a celibate community, and we observe a rule
of silence. I smile at friends in the corridors, and we
signal with our fingers during meals. It's surprising
how much you can tell about someone, even in conditions of silence. Some women have been here a long
time. They say Hypatia, the crone who has the best
room up in the attic with windows opening to the
sea, has been here since the convent's foundation. At
present I'm only a postulant, and when I'm separated
from the others I'm allowed to talk. I chatter away to
Chloe. We two, mother and daughter, lead lives apart
from the community that itself is set apart from the
world.

In a pamphlet, tied on a string to the desk in the hall
for casual visitors or prospective members to browse, I
read that some historians trace our foundation back to
Penthesilea herself. At the end of her reign, and tired
out by pitched battle against men, she saw the need for
a place of retreat for women exhausted like her by
war's high cost in dead and wounded. Women have
followed her here over the years; the island's reputation

as a refuge and a bastion of a certain kind of harmony has grown steadily. New inmates arrive every week, by one means or another. Some of the community are very young girls; they have anticipated the barbarities of the clash and have chosen disengagement. On an island of women there are other forms of conflict; but the special, terrible sore of sexual antagonism can't be rubbed raw here.

I'd woken on the beach, with an abrupt premonition of calamity. Yet blueness lay like a glaze on the sea, sunlight vibrated in the air when I opened my eyes; through my drowsiness, Chloe, wielding a spade in the channel of her sandcastle, where the sea lapped and ebbed, lapped and ebbed, was blue-edged and fiery against the sky, her curly head fringed with light. I smiled at her as I shook the snowblindness out of my eyes and shrugged at the feeling of fear. So many portents of horror fill my dreams – then as now – that in spite of soothsayers' advice I don't care to chase after their meaning. But that day, while Chloe crowed with joy over the flooding moat, a sense of disaster returned. First I noticed that Chloe's things, which I'd left on the boat, were lying beside us in a neat wicker hamper: her shorts, her sunhat, her waterwings. Then, faster, I took in my own suitcase too, packed and standing beside my sunmat. I leapt to my feet, I ran to the sea. How cool and pure the water was, and how fouled and burning I was with the pain. There was no sign of the swooping swallow of his boat. He'd gone, fulfilling those fears that beset me every night in the boat when I

ran away with him, not telling my father. Even while
agreeing to stow me away, even while kissing me, T.
never convinced me that he loved me. I nagged him
for reassurance. But I never found that peace when
you're certain that something is set true in its place.
The uneasiness of his avowals reminded me of my
impatience when a pattern I'm working on the loom
won't come out right, when a discrepancy continues
between the idea of the weave in my head and the
image that appears in the cloth. T. answered my pleas
obliquely: if I flirted with him, he'd pick up my very
words and repeat them: 'T., I am pretty, aren't I? You
do find me pretty, don't you?' (It makes me squirm
now, to remember such cajolery, the self-abasement
that here, on the island, we discard as part of the abandoned order!) And he'd say, 'Yes, you're a pretty little
thing, and I'm a lucky sod.' I'd still feel unsatisfied,
gnawed by shame at my own faked playfulness and
riven with doubts that T. only repeated my banter
because he was at a loss for words.

But he needed me, and I, in my fool's rapture of
surrender, thought that his need bound him to me
with the power of loyalty and trust and delight. He'd
arrived, knowing no one, and at the first dinner in my
father's house he attached himself to me. I knew the
language, the customs of the place, and besides, my
father is a man with influence. T. being older (there
was grey in the hair above his ears and his forehead
was, I noted with a suppressed giggle the first evening,
the shape of a butterfly, with wings at the receding

temples), I didn't immediately fear his approaches. His look of disorientation in a new, foreign place made him appear tractable.

In our family, the dangerousness of men has always been taught as gospel. My mother has suffered so much that now she lives only in darkened rooms. If a candle flame comes near her face she shields herself. She's ravaged by remorse; the taut wrinkles and strained web of skin around the eyes and mouth show how much she has suffered for the notorious passions of her past, and my father preys on her guilt to keep her will in bondage to his. I used to fight him about this: once I even hit him, drubbing his chest with my fists. I wanted to free my mother from his commands, his teasing, his constant cruel jokes. Now I see that as he was betrayed by her, so he became vengeful.

My sister and I used to whisper together from our beds at nights about the sufferings my mother had undergone at the hand of my father and of her many lovers; we vowed never to let it happen to us. We planned to toy with men until, like shrews squealing under the cat's butting, sheathed paw, they'd scurry about terrified of the moment when we'd spread our talons and tear them to bits. We whooped, stifling our cries in the pillow; with the beauty of our young bodies as a weapon we envisaged worlds of torture for men. Tally for tally, we'd exchange cruelties; it was innocence that made us fail to see the great fear of men that was lodged inside us.

T. told me how he loved the possessions of women,

the objects associated with them. How he liked to see
bottles arranged on a dressing table, to open and sniff
them, reminders of cheeks and napes and the underside
of wrists; becoming more daring, how he liked to
follow after a woman in a bathroom, and to smell in
the moist condensing atmosphere her vanished presence, and to find her curled pubic hairs in the bathtub,
to pick them out of the plughole and smell her dis-
carded, stained underclothes on the floor.

I'd never heard a man speak of women as T. did. I
believed he liked us deep down, thoroughly liked us. I
shuddered at his words, half in horror at the breached
intimacies, half in dirty pleasure at my own secret
stains and smells.

All my training to the contrary, I fancied he was on
my side.

In truth I'd been won over to his side by his way of
speaking to me, his promises of worlds of closeness
and mutual enterprise. I no longer saw him as an adversary, one of the enemy tribe who'd brought about my
mother's ruin.

Instead of whispering about imagined battles in the
dark to my sister, I now dreamed of surrender: the
rage that had blazed with such mischief in me I now
saw as monstrous, a beast of malignant and dangerous
stupidity, like the deformed, slobbery brother my dear
mother bore after one of her men abused her credulous-
ness.

So, with my loyal help, T. slew the Minotaur, my
brother. This is of course the famous part of my story

as it is usually told: T's exploits. But what was important to me was that when he came out of the labyrinth at the end of the silken thread that had kept him alive inside that deep, cellular lair of my brother's, he seemed my ally, my champion. I had become essential.

I felt so close to him I cried for happiness, and with those tears I felt that I'd thawed the enmity that had made me scorn all men before. Another monster had been tamed, the monster of my misanthropy; T., guided by a thread of my own weaving, had walked down into the nexus of my terrors and laid them.

But now I was standing on the shore scanning the empty sea until the dazzle of its shifting surface began to make me sick with staring. I thought, he's sailed round the promontory for a fairer anchorage – a storm's foretold – he's sought shelter – he's gone fishing for mackerel for supper, to spike them later on the beach on fennel stalks – he's gone for tackle to a chandler's somewhere – he's gone for a sail, just for a sail, for pleasure.

Chloe, like a dog at the scent of rain, felt my dismay and clutched my legs. We must go, back to the village, we must ask if anyone has seen the boat. Where has Daddy gone? Mummy, has Daddy gone? Good. (She wants me to herself, she has me now for herself.) Is he never coming back? No, no, of course he's coming back. Knowing inside that it wasn't so; the lie choking me. He won his glory with my help; he's the hero, the slayer of my dear, monstrous brother the Minotaur, poor brother, innocent of the crime of your progenitors. Dear brother, I've wronged you by conspiring in your death. And I thought he'd slain my enmity too! I scrabbled in the sand, around the hamper and case. No note from T. Pain began to spill out of me, I was breaking apart at my seams, black pitch on fire seeping out, crackling on my dry surfaces. My love for ever, T.'d said, for ever.

Now, I hope no one will ever feel the pain I felt. Now, I know that the betrayal of love is quite in the order of things, of things outside our order here. On the beach at that moment I wanted everything to feel it with me: I wanted everything around me to die; I wanted the sun to go in and the breeze to stop its playful little caresses; I hated the few carefree puffs of cloud. I wanted to die myself; I dragged myself towards the buildings of the convent on the rise above the beach, rang for admittance, and begged for a room. The portress who answered my call put her finger to her lips, and showed me to my room. Understanding my state, she took Chloe by the hand and drew her away.

Through the week that followed, one or other sister in the community brought me elixirs of hot lemon and honey, and gradually the sensation that I was bleeding fire began to fade. Though the pain remained stuck inside me, as if I'd swallowed it, I was able to see more clearly that I could survive even the abandonment of T. And I wanted Chloe. I longed to see her and hug her and make amends to her for the terrible despair I'd felt.

Then Chloe came in and patted my arm and put her cheek to it, saying she was so glad I was better and would I get up now, and come and play?

So it was Chloe, my daughter, who began to tug me back into the light.

We were beachcombing one day soon afterwards, down by the water in the creek at the bottom of our land, where the stream, carrying the fresh water of the mountains through the orchards, runs into the sea over the sand in a web of rivulets. We were tramping upstream, with our haul of shells and pebbles. I was counting for her the spills and falls from one level to another as the water made its leaping way down to the sea, and, true to my newly stirred maternal conscience, I was instructing her in aspects of our surroundings, explaining how when you're lost you can always follow a stream in the direction of the current, for it will take you to a river, and a river will most likely take you to a town, or, if it doesn't, it will take you to the sea and maybe to a port, and then to . . . freedom.

I was rambling; and Chloe chivvied me, with a child's imperiousness. But I was listening to the water. I can't describe how beautiful the sounds of it are in our garden. It runs off the range of mountains behind us and begins to flow through conduits of terracotta tiles from the high terrace where the soft fruits ripen in the sun, down to the tomato vines and cucumber beds, and then through the lips of a grinning Medusa into a big cistern that brims over continually, a luminous veil spilling down through the mossy cushions that can survive in this hot place through the sheer abundance of the snowmelt. The cistern is one of my favourite places; the lilies' hoof-shaped leaves float there, and at our approach, however stealthy, the bright frogs, green as spring buds freshly unfurled, leap into the water with a neat splash and a streak of skinny divers' legs and flippers. The lapping of little waves, set up by their massed vanishing act, reverberates on the surface of the water, in a series of shining rings. In the whole garden, water, composed of silence and darkness, erupts into music and dazzle at the contact of the thousands of living creatures here; the dazzle seems the echo of the sounds. From the cistern, the spouting conduit carries the stream to the orchard, and babbles past the persimmon trees; then down to the lemon and orange groves below the house, nearer the sea.

My reverie over the water music in my ears was suddenly interrupted. Chloe clutched my hand and shrieked: Mummy, listen. A monster! She tucked herself against my legs. The roar she'd heard came again.

Chloe ran ahead, running back up the stream and then stopping near the lemon trees to locate the direction of the beast's cry. She then turned sharply, making for the eucalyptus grove which screens the convent's midden from view. It's a hideous spot, and all the more shocking after the flecked and fallow light in the gardens, to find under the tall, creaking trees, with their hospital smell and bark peeling off like sunburn, a heap of rubbish slewed this way and that in plastic bags of lurid dye.

Chloe was screaming, half in excitement, half in terror. My brother was leaping on the refuse heap and rootling in the rubbish with his wide mouth. He tore one bag open and began chomping the decaying trash inside; then he spotted us and bounded, in delight at his freedom. Chloe had never seen the Minotaur before; she was born ten months after T. penetrated to the heart of the labyrinth. She hid in my legs and snatched peeps at him.

He let out a hoarse whinny and, fixing us with his sharp, caper-like eyes fringed with white lashes, he butted me on the thigh with his dark, cracked hoof, and threw his great head back in the air. I pulled Chloe off the ground on to my hip and called to my brother like a dog, 'Down, down'. He snorted again, and butted me so hard I rolled to the ground.

Then I saw what T. meant when he boasted that he'd destroyed the Minotaur. On the white fur of the beast's stomach snaked a new, pink scar, where T. had spayed him.

The Minotaur whinnied over us, but didn't harm us. He pushed us with his hooves until we scrambled to our feet again, and tossing his shaggy head until the wattle-like crop on his chest shook, he turned and began to lead us on, towards the tomato vines. He walked with one hock in the small of his back, cramp from his wound stiffened his gait. It was odd to see his powerful frame, his almost puppy-like vitality, constricted, and the new swayback weakness of his spine. He tore the tomatoes roughly from their stalks, pulped them under his hoof and then sucked them dry, and threw the skins on the ground. Then he lumbered off towards the sea, and we followed. He waited for us to catch up and we made our way together.

I looked past the Minotaur's head; we were near the sweet-smelling melon beds, and on the sea the waves gleamed silver under the high August sun's arc lamp. At that moment, there came floating towards us on the light sea breeze a cloud of thistledown. Silky motes wafted by, so light that even Chloe's tiny hand reaching to catch one made enough wind to send it hurtling upwards. Like parachutists, the heavier spores on their glinting threads landed with accelerating force, their flight abruptly ended with a jolt. Some were trying to seed themselves in the Minotaur's shaggy coat; we brushed them off him, laughing.

It was our first contact.

From then on, we began to be entertained by his roughness. He became a necessary companion to us, a kind of court jester, loathsome and lovable, powerful and put-upon at the same time.

There have been times since, when I looked at him and longed for him to crush me in his matted, fetid pelt. Yet he showed no inclination for this. I was curious, and also revolted by him. I'd find myself stealing looks at his muzzle, with its soft, down-covered dewlaps and the coarse whiskers sprouting like sea marram in the duny pinkness of his flesh. Sometimes a slick of saliva covered his wet nose, and he'd slobber. Viscous drips would hang from the overlapping folds of his jaw and catch in the curls of his chest. His total beastliness of appearance was fascinating; my image of the male, the reflection of his tormentor's inner soul, the Minotaur filled me full of thrilling disgust.

I used to be shy of looking at him closely. I kept my eyes averted when I slipped the bolts on the portcullis of the lair we built later for his safety (crows used to fly down at sunset and peck at his eyes, to test his reflexes). But gradually he inspired me to look at him without fear. He won my attentiveness, by his companionable silences on our walks, by his humorous show of strength, by the stench of the robbed virility which still clings to his fur and shows in the packed weave of the musculature on his back, and the flanks, and the splendid rig of his bones.

I became dependent on him.

That summer and early autumn I told the Minotaur, my brother, the story of my love for T., in many versions with different details, different emphases, different questions. Had I made a mistake when I . . . ? Should I have counted on . . . ? What did T. mean when he said . . . ? Should I have understood that . . . ? How could I have helped him to harm my brother? – we also spoke of that. The Minotaur was a good listener, and on the translucent evenings, with the dark blue night glowing through the branches and tatters of moonlight falling on us, I'd sit over a bottle of wine and my monster would then ease himself on to the wrought-iron chair as I told him the worst bits, the bits that had to wait for Chloe's sleep. How I once found T. at my basin, washing the streaks of my juices and his from the soft, cyclopean worm of his shrunken penis with an expression of total repulsion. He already wanted, even then, to go back to his boat, to the smutty talk of men alone together.

As I poured out my rancour in reminiscence, the Minotaur grew bigger and bigger. His compact weight grew denser, until it was no longer safe for him to lean on the wrought iron of my balcony. He increased in size, not rangily, like a human child, but solidly, growing thicker and thicker. I used to cry into my wineglass when I told him how T.'s falseheartedness had made me cleave to him the more. Sometimes my crying made my monster brother clamber up from the floor and lay his burdensome, drooling head in my lap. It was a comfort, to have his pity.

One night I woke, shaken, to find myself slumped across the table of the terrace, with my half-filled wineglass in front of me. My crying was still sticky and dry on my cheeks. I took in the picture of my life with disgust; only then I realised the terrace was still swaying, that the motion wasn't taking place in a dream or in my head. For a few moments, the shadows of the interlaced leaves blurred; the building swung from the sky. My Minotaur dragged himself up the steps, whining. He'd grown so heavy he could hardly move. I held the scruff of his mane for anchorage and waited for the shaking world to find its balance again.

The sky continued to clear in the days that followed,

deep as a star sapphire. But because I felt the unpredict-
able, steamy earth was dangerous for Chloe, we began
to make our daily excursions by boat. We had a
smooth, carvel-built dinghy, with four oars and a short
mast; my brother Minotaur soon learned to use the
oars, and the three of us would row or sail out to a
humpbacked island Chloe called the Dinosaur, and
have a picnic there, on the rocky shore that hadn't
gaped open.

Chloe was paddling with her shrimping net in the
shallows; I was reading, with my back against a sun-
warmed rock. It was Chloe who first saw you. I looked
up and saw you too, a small, dark speck in the
gorgeous multicoloured balloon as bright and banded
as a spinnaker in full sail, with flames shooting from a
brazier in the basket beside you, fuelling the golden-
red orb above you. You were moving in the swinging
basket beneath the balloon, reducing the intensity of
the flames, I realise now, as you began to make your
descent into . . . our garden.

We ran for our boat. Helter-skelter, we pulled our
belongings together and threw them in; the Minotaur
pushed us off, dragging himself on the sharp shingle
under water up to his waist so we could straightaway
pick up the wind. I hoisted the little sail and we made
for our beach. The balloon skimmed the eucalyptus,
the tallest trees in the garden, and bumped to ground.
It bounced and swayed on its guy ropes, then gradually
deflated, settling in swirling fall upon fall of colour.

We couldn't see you; only the collapsing magnificence of your transport.

Chloe ran to greet you; I threw down the remains of the picnic in the kitchen, and quickly pulled a shift over myself and put a band in my hair to hold it tidy. Then I joined you by the balloon. You were laughing, do you remember? You were laughing because Chloe was so excited her questions were tumbling out pell-mell and you hadn't a moment to answer her. She was spell-bound by the balloon, lying stretched out by the lily pond over the herb garden. The smell of basil, crushed by your alighting, was overwhelming. When you saw me, you nodded, and brought your lips together in a smile, no longer a wide laugh.

I bowed back. My heart leapt at the sight of you. It had been a long time since I'd seen a man. I was ashamed at myself for being pleased, so I spoke as severely as I could. 'You must leave. You are forbidden to land here. It's private property.'

You apologised, but stood your ground and made no move. You pointed to the crushed basil plants. 'They'll recover soon enough,' you said, cheerfully.

I didn't answer; I remembered I should observe the rule of silence, especially to an invader. You began gathering up the folds of the balloon. But Chloe flung herself down and rolled in the heavy, painted canvas and giggled.

You let the attempted folds go, and spoke to me again.

You told me you were a botanist, and you were

sailing over these islands trying to discover the migration routes of flower spores; how wild flowers and plants were disseminated through the air by the prevailing breezes. The spring and autumn were important seeding times. You pointed to the motes, afloat in the air.

You weren't allowed, as a man, to stay in our community. I told you that. Strictly speaking, you should have left the island straight away. Your presence was as seismic as the tremors that had shaken us a few nights before you landed.

A meeting was called that night, in the great hall of the convent, to discuss your case. Many of my sisters were filled with bitterness against me for my tolerance of such a breach of our pact as women; when you said you wanted to study and intended no harm, one of my sisters whistled in disbelief. But Hypatia, our oldest member, suggested you be put to a simple test, and if you passed it you should be allowed to stay, outside the boundary of our convent, until you'd completed your work on the island, and that then you should be allowed to depart unharmed. 'We have no quarrel with men who have no quarrel with us,' she said, her voice hoarse and small with lack of use. 'Men invented warfare; we do not want to imitate their ways.' In order to prove your pledges of friendship with the female, she desired to interrogate you before our tribunal.

I was afraid for you; I couldn't believe any man would be capable of responding satisfactorily to the questioning of our great lady. And, already, I didn't want to see you go.

Many in our community knew my weakness; Hypatia told me I would never rise to full sisterhood. 'You are made for the world, Ariadne. Stay with us a while. Heal yourself. Then go.'

Courteously Hypatia asked you about ownership, maternity, autonomy; these were easy questions, and you acquitted yourself well. But you could have been lying. After all, on an island founded by Amazons, what man would be such an idiot as to deny a woman's rights – to choose to be a mother, to control her children, to own land and wealth independently. But then, clasping the arm of her curule chair, Hypatia folded her transparent, knotty fingers, and leaned forward to ask you, 'Who is superior, the man or the woman?'

You didn't think long. My heart flew to my mouth. I thought, a man will say a man, if he is telling the truth as he sees it; but if he is seeking to please the tribunal he will say 'a woman', and we will know he lies.

You spread your hands and said shyly, 'Can I use a figure of speech, instead of a straight answer?' Hypatia nodded. You went on. Your voice was matter-of-fact and quiet. 'In botany, the science I study, there's a common phenomenon, known to us as enantiomorphosis.' (There was a scornful titter, but you carried on.) 'Indeed, the phenomenon is widespread in nature, occurring in all creatures as well as in plants. On a vine the tendrils twist one way as they leave the stem; they twist another way to fasten themselves; in the centre, where they meet, the spirals stop, and the join shows no kink.'

Hypatia's dry fingers scraped lightly on the chair. 'Yes, yes, we're attending to you. To the point,' she said.

You spoke of the horns of a deer, their mirrored similarity one to another, of pairs of tusks, of pairs of wings, then you held up your hands to us, in a gesture of proffering and said, 'There's no difference of degree between my left hand and my right. They're the same, but completely distinct.'

There was another titter at this: one of the younger women heckled, 'There's one thing that you've only got one of!'

'Yes,' another cried, laughing. 'That doesn't come in pairs!'

Hypatia tapped the arm of her chair, scoldingly, and nodded to you to continue. You went on, 'A man and a woman aren't mirror images of each other, like clockwise spirals or counter-clockwise spirals. We're different and we can't ever be the same, and there's no superiority or inferiority in our difference. When we join, we join as neatly as clasped hands, or tendrils forming a straight link.'

A light smile played round Hypatia's lips. A murmur rose in the hall, punctuated by some whistling.

'It's a fair reply,' Hypatia interrupted. She asked for

a show of hands to decide whether you should be allowed to complete your research. The motion was carried, by three votes; and although some of my sisters who voted against you grumbled and cold-shouldered me for my initial breach of the convent rules, they accepted the decision gallantly.

In the days that followed, while you surveyed the island's flowers and entered your findings in various charts, Chloe became your constant companion. I wondered that my acceptance of solitude hadn't cramped her young life. Acceptance of solitude? Acceptance of separateness. We hadn't been alone.

Chloe was avoiding my brother, the Minotaur, too. He pined for her. I could tell how much he minded the interrupted intimacy of our former evenings. For now, after supper on the terrace, I went indoors and read in bed, while you finished the day's note-taking in your quarters in the village.

I was very alert these night-time hours; drink no longer stupefied my faculties. I was on the watch; I longed for your footfall one night outside my door.

The Minotaur was diminishing before my eyes and I didn't care. You never commented on his decline; in fact, until I began writing this, I'm not certain you ever really noticed our Minotaur.

Then one night, talking over dinner, I decided that when you relit the fire in your balloon and left for the next landing-place to which winds would take you, Chloe and I would leave as well.

You looked at me, I could hardly hold my face up to the blaze of your pleasure.

So we left the island, after I paid a goodbye visit to Hypatia high in her attic and received her quiet, wry blessing, and we landed on the next island of the archipelago, where we live now. It was only later that I realised that in my new life I hadn't noticed that something – someone – who'd always been with me had gone. At first I groped to understand the unexpected feeling of loss. How in the midst of such happiness and love could I feel a gap, where something familiar once flourished? Was the love I felt for you flawed already? Yet I was so close to you and Chloe in those days, as if the planes of our several existences had curved to make one smooth sphere, that I found it difficult even to concentrate on pursuing the meaning of this twinge, this absence. It cost me an effort, but I finally found the cause. Of course, how could I have forgotten? It was my Minotaur's constant, bulky shadow I'd lost: my companion in rancour, the foil to my wallowing self-abasement. I'd shed him, my other self, my monster of loathing.

One night I woke up, jolted again in my sleep by a spasm of the earth. This time I was in bed with you. You sleep deeply and though you turned, the tremor didn't wake you. I slipped out of bed and went out into the night.

The horizon was glowing, in the direction of the island of women. I stood on the shore and watched a golden sheaf of sparks fan out and fall into the sea. As

the red glow died, rings of water swelling from far
away eventually reached us here with a gentle rasp,
depositing on our strand a residue of dry light clinkers,
a honeycombed charnel.

I wrote to the convent; to my relief, a letter came
back swiftly, saying that all was well, that a small
earthquake had shaken the northern shore. The sea had
reclaimed the tip of that promontory, but the convent
had stood firm. There was nothing in the letter about
the Minotaur.

Chloe picked up one of the clinkers the other day,
when we were walking on the beach, and showed me
its skull-like bosses and holes. I suggested to Chloe she
keep it for a hopscotch stone, but she said it wasn't
smooth enough.

On the island, my experience had been common.
Indeed T. figured more honourably than many of the
other men at whose hands my convent sisters – and my
mother – had suffered. I only knew there the love that
takes pain's part and fosters it. But you've shown me a
love that knows the meaning of pain so well it uses it
with proper scorn.

On the island, many of the community think that
love between man and woman is impossible; the love
of children remains, and the loving friendship of
women together. But the love of the sexes is merely an
excuse to exploit women's fruitfulness for the ends of
the patriarchy.

I can't make my life fit any one gospel; I'm an apos-
tate to the community I shared for a time. If I could

describe how fruitfulness of the soul grows in contingency and how much more fruitful I am, in my own eyes, contingent upon you, I would write it. Instead, I sent the community a copy of this record of my feelings. Many say that the story of Ariadne ended when you came to the island and carried me off. But Hypatia will know the falsehood of that. For me and for Chloe your coming was the first moment, and no amount of wordshed can match our sequel's tide.

Now You See Me

(After Veronese's *Susannah and the Elders*)

The night is full of noises: the chatter of birds and the whirr and zing of insects. With your eyes shut you can feel the trees closing in on the house, pressing up against the roof eaves and the veranda balustrade, their boughs astir. But your eyelids parting in the first pale humid light, you can then see again how sparsely the trees grow and can't make out the bright woodpecker or the chafing insects that seem so near. When you pull yourself from your bed to look out more carefully, the dew on the lawn is glittering and the kells like crystal hammocks hang from springing blade to blade. You know it's going to be hot, as hot as it can be in that enclave of gardens and suburban houses cordoned off from the boom city on the peninsula.

You. No, I. *I* knew it was going to be hot. I stepped slowly, the heat already flattening the breath in my body, my footsteps on the boards of my bedroom, Man Friday prints of dark sweat on the sheen. I often call myself you, as you do. I think of myself as 'you', as I go about things from day to day. Susannah, what a fool you are to eat one more piece of bread for breakfast in the morning than you resolved. You'll never lose weight if you carry on like that.

I was happy seeing myself through others' eyes (your eyes), watching that 'you' move and walk and sleep. I was happy to be outside myself, standing in your sight, to be 'you' when we were together and when we were apart until – but you shall hear.

Joachim had left for town when I got up; he rises early so that he can return at lunchtime and lie down during the dog heat of the day. The towel in the bathroom was still wet from his shower. Nothing dries here. I took another towel from the store; I turned on the shower; the jet refreshed me. I wished the school term had not begun again, as I drank my coffee and refused the bread the amah offered me, the light, wholesome bread that represents the best legacy of the European power that colonised this country. With the children still on holiday, I could put off doing the firm's accounts; we could drive to the windward side of the peninsula and sit together in the lapping air and guess as each wave swelled, Would it make the beach and spill itself there? Dan would pick one breaker; Seth another, their mother a third. But she was watching absently, often forgetting to follow her chosen contender with her eyes, for they were drawn away from the rolling ocean by the straight, smooth limbs of her sons. Oh, that was yours, Seth would say with disgust, as his mother's choice unfurled its scalloped banner over the sand. 'Was it, darling? I don't think so.' 'And you're not even playing properly,' Dan, furious, remonstrated at his mother's try at diplomatic defeat. 'It was yours. You're pretending it wasn't so Seth can win.' More disgust, bodies looped together on the sand; separating, down by the water again. 'Look a crab! It'll get you.' They ran past her, ablaze in the light that was shaken off the sea's shifting facets, oblivious of her, of the laughter and the pride the sight of them stirred in her eyes.

I remember the end for me of that Edenic stage when shame had no place and I never looked upon myself to see myself with the eyes of others. I was eight: Seth will be eight next year, Dan is one year younger. My mother brought the coat of a guest to her bedroom, and caught me red-handed, out of bed and making up in her mirror. I was transfixed by the perfect lopped cylinder of her lipstick, as if her mouth had sliced the tip sideways like a salami. I was trying right up against the glass to stiffen my lips into a shape that would fit the smooth end, but the breath misted the mirror, my hand slipped, and smeared like an infant who's gorged at the jampot, I was discovered. My heart beat with fear, but my mother laughed. She wiped off the scarlet mess and told me, as my punishment for getting out of bed and being so vain, I must come downstairs. There, I was to recite to her friends the poem I'd told her I'd learned by heart.

I didn't want to. The faces of her friends, cigarettes and hairstyles, corrugated eye pouches, thread veins and pungent fragrances of hair lotion, women's perfume, assailed me. I backed up against the books on the shelves and stared up past their attending phalanx to look at the words printed in my head:

'I will let loose against you the fleet-footed vines–
I will call in the Jungle to stamp out your lines!
  The roofs shall fade before it,
    The house-beams shall fall,
  And the *Karela*, the bitter *Karela*
    Shall cover it all!'

Mowgli had watched the people whose settlements marched with the jungle and encroached; they had not spied on him, let alone watched him. But I was watched.

I concentrated on the spool of spinning print in my mind's eye; but I still saw them as they watched me and though I found it uncomfortable, even excruciating, to be the focus of their eyes, I wanted terribly to please, to please them and to please my mother. When I ended and they clapped and clucked and cooed and exclaimed, 'Frances, darling, what a memory your little girl's got!' I detected a note of respect, but not pleasure. They were impressed by the child reciting, mouth a round O of enmity like a perverted chorister, but they did not warm to me. ('You're nothing but a big fat idiot, Susannah, you choose a poem like that and then you want people to like it and to love you . . . What do you expect?')

In the kitchen, the amahs were quarrelling, they are always yapping at each other, baring gold teeth and

smoothing their hair over brow and skull, wretchedly
working back and forth like hired mourners. Usually I
try and part them by assigning them to different tasks
or, in my pidgin, try to discover the cause of their
falling out and bring about a reconciliation; but today,
with the heat stacked on the lip of the coming day
about to spill its load like a storm cloud, I couldn't bear
the shrill and squealing misery of their strife. I called
out. They came, gesturing their mutual antipathy and
murmuring imprecations. I told them to take the day
off. 'Holidays,' I said. They did not look altogether
pleased; to be relieved of a day's work robbed them of
the intense pleasure of recriminating all day together.

But I wanted silence – and solitude.

The women left. I tilted the slats so that light fell on
to the table where I do Joachim's accounts; I sat down
to the work without relish. We have to keep the books
scrupulously, else the new government will use slip-
shod accountancy as a pretext to take over assets of
foreign companies like ours. The columns must show
materials we have imported, materials we have bought
locally, wages we have paid. I have to enter the same
sets of figures four or five times: in the records of
the individual contract or building, in the different tax
books, direct and indirect, in the client's book, in the
company's book for the client's records, and for our
company's annual accounts. It's the kind of work I
wish I wasn't good at; the struggle I have between
doing it nimbly and finding it so dull wears me out.

The sweat stood out on my forehead and rolled into

my eyes. I wiped it back into my hair. I made notes on the items that exceeded Joachim's estimate for the new hotel on the leeward side. I flapped my blouse to inflate it, and felt soothed as it slowly emptied and settled again, cooling me a touch. I made a separate set of calculations, working out how the excess on the tiles round the hotel pool could be lost on other items. (They'd come from Italy, 20 per cent over budget.) It's too hot to work, Susannah, it's too hot.

I lifted a slat between my fingers. Light was moving on the grass without glints: the dew dry already.

You could lie under the flame tree, in the shade, Susannah, with a book. There's no one here. You'll be screened by the fence. I dropped the blind, turned back to the ledgers. Enough for one morning.

I peeled off my blouse and stepped under the shower again, rinsing the salt of my sweat out of my hair, holding the jet to sluice the stickiness. Pit and crutch, don't forget, as my mother used to say.

The rattan mat unrolled under the scarlet spires of the broad-leaved tree was fresh to the contact of my skin; I stripped off my clean blouse and skirt and lay back in the dapple. But the film of warmth that clung to all forms clothed me the next instant, enfolding anything that interrupted the soft density of space, my body too alongside all the other shapes that lifted and moved the soft heavy air, the humming insects, the disclosed blooms, the birds that flopped rather than darted in amongst the leaves.

Joachim had made love to me as soon as the guests

of the night before had gone; he had needed no encouragement from me. They had excited him, and I'd accepted his greedy taking of me for himself, although his desire had only been fanned by theirs. It wasn't the first time that Joachim had said, before some business associates arrived to eat with us, 'Put on something, well, you know, something . . .' and then described curves in the air, the contours of imagined breasts and hips. We ate in the garden, with the mosquito candles smoking. There were two guests. One, the representative from the Belgian property company that has won the concession for the new racecourse (as if the colony's needs weren't met by the old course in the hills), was a handsome man of a florid, fleshy sort, with grey curls swept back and wet on the nape of his sunburned neck. Dierek laughed easily, with a loud, urgent wholeheartedness that at first I found pleasant. The second man, an Italian, was the architect, Saldieri, and I'd seen his award-winning design for the grandstand in the local press. It was graceful and ingenious. He's adapted the traditional construction with bamboo timber and bamboo leaf thongs to enamelled steel in the European high-tech style. It was easier for me at first to talk to him than to his employer's representative. But later things turned out differently. Saldieri was a reticent man with a brooding forehead and dark eyes, which, for all their size and depth of colour, were oddly empty at contact. He made little dents in the tablecloth with his nails as he strummed.

Joachim wanted the site contract even more than

he'd wanted to build the new hotel, and I was to help him. 'Susannah, I have to build so much shit. These plans are beautiful. I'd never look back – we'd never look back if I built that grandstand. And I can do it. The workforce has never been better; the foreman's got them eating out of his hand. It will be perfect. Saldieri himself will be amazed at the quality of the work out here. You must help me to persuade them. You must.'

Before they came last night, he looked me over and twitched his lips with appreciation. 'You are beautiful, Susannah,' he said.

I'm proud of Joachim. He's an adventurer, but without the adventurism. He came out here on an inspiration when he could have stayed riskless at home, and he learned the language and the byways of the country's customs with speed and energy until the natural suspicion and xenophobia of a once-colonised zone evaporated and government and commerce liked to deal with him. But I flinched at the way he looked at me as he considered the effect I would have on the resistance of Dierek and Saldieri. I flinched first and then I warmed. Joachim's eyes aren't empty, but mischievous, and the sex mischief in them when he looked me over buzzed inside me till I giggled.

The evening had continued like that; when my butterfly sleeve dropped off my shoulder as I poured Saldieri some mineral water he wanted, I let it fall and even stretched my neck to set off the bareness of my shoulder. Saldieri watched, but said nothing. Dierek did: to Joachim, he said, 'Your wife is a splendid woman, Joachim.' And then, exploding with laughter, 'Thank God for Caucasian women, eh, Paolo! The little girls downtown –' and he pulled his bright eyes until they slitted '– are fine for an hour, but . . . Yes, you're a lucky devil, Joachim. She's splendid.'

I was glad when it was over, when Joachim undressed me brusquely and sank into me with as much necessity as if we'd been caressing each other for hours.

I turned on the rattan, and tried to pitch myself back from slumber into the day. Something soft touched my cheek. A daytime moth. I put my hand up to brush her away, gently, and a hand closed round mine and a voice said, 'Hello, Susannah. Hello there.'

I tried to cover myself with one arm and held out the other hand to Saldieri, who stood there as serious as the night before, to take my shirt back from him. I think it was a plea too, that gesture. He held it out to me, but did not let go. I jumped up and pulled the rattan with me, like a shield; Dierek stepped behind me and laughed. 'Joachim,' I cried, 'Joachim is coming back.'

Dierek spluttered on his guffaw. 'He's meeting us here,' he said. 'He had invited us to lunch, didn't he tell you?'

Saldieri let go my hand and cupped my face. 'In half an hour, Susannah.' He intoned my name. 'A lot can happen in half an hour.' And he took his hand from my face and lifted the rattan like a curtain and looked me up and down.

You're a splendid woman, Susannah, they want to feast on you because you're beautiful. Aren't you proud of being beautiful? Show them, Susannah, let them in, your husband will be pleased and proud that his friends understand how fortunate he is, won't he?

Think, how flattering, your beauty overpowers them. You're not moved, and they are weak and wanting you. What's there to fear? Dance for them, Susannah, show them a leg and more, they'll clutch at you and fall on all fours for a touch, you could make them eat out of the palm of your hand.

Cry, Dirty bastards, tighten your contempt till it matches their look and breaks them, hurt them with your coldness, hit out where they mind. Call them no-good rapists. Where are your balls? Call that a cock?

But remember your mother, yes. I wish you'd learn to be more gracious. Yes. There's nothing in the world as unattractive as foul language in a woman. Yes. Do try and be more feminine, darling. Yes. That's better. Yes. Good, darling. And pity. Don't forget pity. Men need our pity.

In a tropical house, every room gives on to every other without locks, nothing but flimsy partitions. I ran, I began dressing myself; Dierek slid the door and watched. Saldieri passed behind him and came in; I was pulling on some trousers, the first T-shirt I could find.

'Please,' said Saldieri. He held me from behind and began to move against me with scissor-like sawing of his legs, one hand shoving down under my waistband, fingers scrabbling to prise me apart. 'Please, Susannah,' he said again.

Dierek was crouched against the wall and holding himself, stoking himself, up and down, and Susannah, you weren't there any longer, in your skin your bones your flesh, child, no, but in the corner of the ceiling, microscopic and insect-like on the plaster. You were watching. Then Dierek groaned and then his groaning turned to crowing and you Susannah you were watching the little girl performing for the grown-ups. Try and recall it Susannah, what was it, mixed up with your longing that they love you and find you wonderful, what was it? Yes, Susannah, remember, the song against people. And the insect flew down from the ceiling and into your eye, your eye.

How long have you been watching me? How long has my body been inside your eyes? How long has my ordinary flesh, my secret part, been yours, how long has your spying on me turned me inside out? I know how perilous the inside of things can be: I know the blue smoothness of the fish when the fishwife guts it for me in the market; the eviscerated carcass on the anatomical plate, fruit and flowers of flesh of the interior turned inside out; the red-black juice of over-ripe tomatoes squashed under careless shoppers' feet; the dentist's intimate medicine-scented finger in my gums and on the silvery underface of my veined cheek; I know the soft crumbly pollution inside gloves. My sons' illnesses turn the inside out, and only the most loved and closest can bear it, the inner body made visible.

You Susannah are being rendered down; your fat and juices are simmering in the round hot cauldron of their wilful eyes. Yes. They are reducing you, Susannah, you are leaking out of your openings and fissures, you are in their gaze, holes and nooks and crannies, nipple a nozzle and mouth a drain, and even your navel opening, and no, no, no, no, the pulpy shell of your vulva is widening widening in their many-tongued look until there's going to be nothing left of you but a round O, Susannah. Let me disappear. Make this dissolution of my self complete until nothing is left of me but my print on the floor. Let me drain away through the good earth where the insects tick and the plumed creatures peck. You have made me nothing by your watching. Let me be nothing.

No! And I bit down on the arm pinning me against the quivering body of the man clamped around me and kicked at his legs behind and stopped him with the sharpness of it from continuing to dabble in me. 'Get out of here,' I shouted, 'Get out.' Then I pushed Saldieri towards the door and shouted to Dierek. He went, wiping himself, and gave me a finger. 'You whore,' he said.

They met Joachim in the garden; he flung an arm around Saldieri and led him back into the house. He

was apologising for keeping them waiting. He hadn't
realised the appointment was so early. Had they had a
drink at least?

Dierek shrugged. 'Susannah was occupied with
something else,' I heard him say.

Saldieri coughed in his dry throat. 'She had a visitor.'

Joachim my husband looked bewildered. His arm
fell from round the men's necks. 'Susannah,' he cried,
'Susannah?'

I waited for him to reach me. 'Tell them to leave us
together,' I said to my husband, and we went indoors.

'Joachim,' I was speaking quietly under my breath.
'They came early, I was in the garden . . .' I choked, I
gestured at my body.

Joachim looked at me. 'What are you saying,
Susannah . . . ?' His face went white; two spots of
colour flamed on his cheeks, on his forehead the sweat
stood out, and he buried his head in my shoulder and
groaned, 'Are you all right?'

'What is she telling you, Ingegnere?' said Saldieri,
when Joachim went out to the two men and asked
them to leave. 'She is lying to you, you poor fool . . .'
And he made the sign of the two-horned beast.

Joachim's eyes wavered back to me, standing on the
veranda.

I came down the steps, slowly. I was shaking.
'Joachim,' I said, 'believe me.'

Joachim looked at me. 'Of course.'

Dierek guffawed.

'Stronzo,' said Saldieri. 'Povero stronzo.'

Dierek said, 'She was in the garden.' And he swivelled his hips lasciviously. 'With a local boy. He jumped over the hedge when he saw us . . . Ask her, see if she can deny it . . .'

Saldieri: 'Yes, he jumped over the wall when he saw us.'

Joachim: 'The hedge? Where? The wall? Where?'

Saldieri's eyes flew round the garden. 'Out of the gate, I mean.'

'But I was driving in . . .' said Joachim.

'Go,' I said, 'go away, you should have more shame.'

I took Joachim by the arm and led him to the house.

Joachim never believed Dierek and Saldieri; sometimes I find him beside me in bed, teeth clenched, with tears of rage standing in his sleepless eyes. 'My wife, they tried to rape my wife . . .' I hold him and try and smooth away the knots and tangles in his spirit.

But once he warned me, 'Susannah, don't ever take your clothes off again, even when you think you are alone.'

So I am to blame; also, I know that the sight of the grandstand's rising scaffolding fills him with rancour. He controls his disappointment, out of respect. But I feel it coiled inside him, sometimes, when he looks at me.

I was walking in the old quarter the other day and I got lost. The stepped alleys defy a European's bump of locality, and it's easy to stray. I turned a corner of the

street near the vegetable market which I thought was
familiar, and I found myself in the courtyard of what
must have been once a grand establishment, now converted into tenements. The temple in the corner was
guarded by lion dogs, washing strung from jaw to jaw.
The children who always surround a roundeye if you
stray jumped around me, some shouting 'Hey! baby'
and 'Cute! Cute!', even 'Cutiepie' – the last phrases
remembered from the war. I tried to cry above their
hubbub for directions back to the market centre, and
they swept me on and into a chamber which was curtained off from the yard. An old lady was sitting there
in the semi-darkness, in silence. She pointed out the
way, and I thanked her, and turned to go. As I turned,
a figure moved behind one of the columns of the building. The child had crept out of cover to take me in. But
she? he? did not move fast enough, and when I saw the
child I cried out.

Sometimes in the East you still see lepers, begging at
the entrances of large gathering places. No doubt one
or two will sit patiently at the gates of the new racecourse, and beg their bread from us as we enter. I don't
know what had deformed the child who stayed within,
beside the silent matriarch in her dark room. She – I do
think of the child as a girl – stopped my heart with
horror, and then, almost instantly, with pity too; but if
she had not ducked away from my sight but grabbed at
me like all the other children of that place, I don't think
I could have put out my hand to take hers or touch her
bloated and disfigured face without recoiling. As it

was, with my coward's shriek, I fell away for a moment from humankind, when I caught a glimpse of a child who had learned to keep away from being watched.

The Legs of the Queen
of Sheba

After the official dinner was over, it was my turn to entertain in my room. I fussed, I hid my underwear under a towel though it was still dripping from the wash, I shifted my spongebag to hide the anti-wrinkle cream and buttonback dispenser of pills, and zipped up my razor. Greg and I took the twin beds; Thomas found a niche on the hotel furniture. Soon, we were talking about legs.

'You're not a legs man, are you?' Thomas challenged Greg.

He acknowledged the truth of this with a solemn swig of the duty-free malt he'd chosen at the airport. 'I don't know what you're meant to look for.'

Thomas grunted, 'Length, of course. Long legs, legs that go on and on.' He sketched this dream in the air, stopping at the cleft.

I turned my head to Greg alongside me on the other bed and said, 'But Danielle has the most beautiful legs ever, surely?' Danielle lives with Greg in Cambridge; she's my friend too, and as neatly turned as one of those ivory lay figurines of Chinese medicine, which were used to point out to the doctor where it hurt by women too modest to expose their own bodies.

I said, pulling up my skirt, 'Now there, Greg, there's a pair of good legs. This is what's meant by legs. The knees should be round, and almost invisible when the leg is straight. So.' I demonstrated, flexing my knee and twirling one foot near Greg's face. 'The ankle should be slender, but not bony. The thighs should be . . .'

Greg looked, and drank, and shook his head.

'I know about arses, too,' volunteered Thomas. 'They should be high and hard.'

'Arses is it?' said Kevin, coming in. 'Makes a change from predicting the student intake in the natural sciences, as I've just been doing, adding the finishing touches for tomorrow's session, while you lot have been revelling, by the looks of things.' He helped himself to a toothmug of malt and found a perch on the radiator shelf by the window.

I went back to lying on top of the other bed, with Greg across the gap from me. 'My mother taught me,' I continued. 'She used to sit around discussing the points of her friends, like trainers sizing up bloodstock. That's what I used to hear when I was a child. "Have you taken a long hard look at her thighs?" – shrieks of laughter – "Her wrists, big like shackles?" – "Tut-tut, they're not as bad as that" – "Her ears?" – hoots – "Those earlobes would look better on a dachshund." Assassination, item by item, not of character, no, but of bodies. A kind of ritual dismemberment.'

Greg said, 'That's a bad strike against your sex, I'm afraid.'

Thomas said, 'Takes a woman to know one.' I drank up, waved the bottle at the boys, took some more.

'I like them smooth,' said Kevin, after a pause.

Thomas said, 'Since when do they come rough?'

'You know, hairy.' Kevin was sleepy, his lids heavy.

'Yeah, black fuzz flattened by the mesh of the tights, I know.'

A bit late, I grasped for loyalty to my own. 'Legs don't feel like they look. Black cats may saunter in and sidle up to Pretty Polly Longlegs in the ads, and rub themselves against her – but you can't touch her in the ad, you can only see her. If you could, you might find you prefer unshaven legs. Like men's, they're softer. Down is nice. With shaving, there's a risk of stubble.'

Thomas grimaced.

Greg said, 'Danielle's always smooth. And I can get into Danielle's bathwater after she's shaved her legs in it. I'm very proud of that. I don't mind the little black bits.'

'She must be good about doing it, often,' I said.

Thomas exhaled, noisily, to show his amusement. And I saw what I'd said; and stopped playing one of the boys.

When they'd gone, I looked at my face in the mirror and watched the tears spring, with a certain grim pleasure that at least I could still feel. You stupid cow, I told my screwed-up mug. You think you can lie there, banter banter, girls this, girls that, you think it makes you liked and clever. Fool. Trade secrets, tell on your own kind, show your legs. Fool. Pretend you're in the know, keep up, egg them on, never dare show you're shocked, never protest. Where they lead, you'll follow. Drink, smoke, vie, boast. Fool. Fool woman, what's worse.

Shame, slimy with tears, had her nails well and truly dug into the stuff of my soul and was clinging on tight, while her grim sisters, drink and no-sex, were sinking their claws into other parts as viciously.

I hadn't even kept faith with myself. My mother with her scorecards of physical perfections had inflicted pain on me during my clumsy, plumpish, brainy adolescence, yet I'd pushed the memory away. My teacher's wisdom had taught me to keep women's codes from men because otherwise they use them to make women their pets, their dollies, their babies. In the classroom I faced day by day the need for girls not to want to please boys. So Shame returned to scratch my face, and I took pleasure watching her make the tears come.

But I did not know then, as I went heavily to bed in the conference hotel in Jerusalem, how closely I had brushed the Queen of Sheba that night.

The Queen of Sheba came from the south and proved King Solomon with hard questions. The sky of my northern city hangs like blackout blinds and I had failed to issue any challenge. '*Nigra sum sed formosa,*' says the Shulamite, Solomon's beloved, in the Song of Songs, the love song of the Queen of Sheba and the King, according to commentaries on the Bible (*I am black, but comely*) – my closeness to her can't be found there either.

Raphael painted her leaping up the shallow steps of the King's dais towards Solomon, while he starts up from his throne to take her in his arms. She flings her right arm behind her to point to the servants in her company, some of whom, stripped like wrestlers to the waist, heave cauldrons of gold coin on their shoulders. One attendant is spilling the contents of his jar on the ground, and another's stooping under the burden of an earthenware pot, filled with some precious liquor. Solomon's beard and hair escape in a grey fleece from the spikes of his oriental diadem. Male wisdom needs years to mature, but the Queen's springs green in her young limbs and eager embrace.

I do not recognise myself here either.

The Queen of Sheba never grows old, unlike Eve. But Eve belongs in her story too, for when the first mother laid Adam out, there grew from the corpse the tree that would grow the wood of the Cross. The Queen of Sheba, daughter of Eve, recognised it many centuries later, in the foothills before Jerusalem, when she reached a bridge made from the tree spanning the stream of Gihon in the valley of Kidron, and refused to set foot upon the instrument of our future redemption. Instead, she knelt to worship it, as Piero painted in his fresco cycle on the legend of the Holy Cross in Arezzo.

Later, when she forded the stream, she lifted her

skirts. And so, on the way to the Temple where Solomon would receive her, she showed her legs.

The valley of Kidron lies to the south of Jerusalem, beneath the south-eastern corner of the walls of the Temple Mount, where we'd been shown by our official Israeli guide the commissure between the masonry of the Second Temple that Herod built and the massive stones hewn in the earlier, Hasmonean era. Today, tobacco grows there, wand-like self-seeded saplings, with perfumed yellow bells in spring. Behind the rampart of golden-rose limestone stand the multiple arcades of the stables called Solomon's, that were used by the Templar knights for their horses when they occupied the holy site. Above, the dome of the Al-Aqsa mosque, the knights' own Temple, rises to twin the golden bowl of the Dome of the Rock; Al-Aqsa's used to be silver, but is now lead. George H., an old hand in Jerusalem, took me inside last time I was here; there was a smell like a boys' changing room.

The Queen of Sheba reached the valley of Kidron and looked up to this view of the city two millennia before tobacco travelled to the Mediterranean, one millennium before the Islamic dome rose over the most contested shrine in the world – but she would have seen her destination, the emplacement of the Temple, when she lifted her skirts to ford the waters, and the Muslims who later occupied the Judaic Holy of Holies and obliterated its precise location still continue to tell the story of the Queen of Sheba's coming. Their storytellers also claim Solomon as one of their own, and intended to magnify the wisdom and glory of the King. A master of djinns, a wizard from whom nothing was hidden, the Solomon of the Koran and later Muslim lore could work prodigies of magic, unscramble the speech of birds, and eavesdrop on the gossip of camels.

Picnicking out in the desert of Judaea one day, under the green shade of Jericho's palms and fruit groves, Solomon summoned the birds, his eyes and hands abroad, to give news of his dominions and further afield. Only one bird did not come. In some stories, the hoopoe is the culprit, in others the lapwing, perhaps a more fitting messenger in this context because of her cunning in survival. For the bird, when she finally answered the King's summons, calmed his rage – temporarily – by telling him of a great wonder she had found in the south, a woman who ruled her country on her own. This Queen from the south was a beauty, and, like Solomon, clever. She was not quite as rich, but not threadbare either. Unlike the King, however, who kept his wives on the mountain of Silwan nearby, the Queen of Sheba, like me, was single.

Solomon's rage against the truant bird gave way to curiosity. He ordered her to return to Sheba with a letter for its Queen, warning her he would advance against her people if she did not submit to his suzerainty. Then he struck camp and returned to Jerusalem, to wait for her reply.

The djinns who served him warned that such a contradiction of the due order might be monstrous. They hinted that such a woman, beautiful, wise, fairly rich, and unwed, might be a sorcerer's illusion, might have hidden diabolical features. Ass's hooves, they whispered; hairy legs, they tittered.

Solomon waited for her answer. He was impatient to know about her; his wives had made him an expert in the subject of women, and experts must prime their expertise to keep up their standards.

In Christian images, when the Queen of Sheba submits to Solomon she shows her wisdom; she shows she's clever enough to understand, in spite of being a heathen and a foreigner and one of the damned who couldn't be saved because they were born before the salvation of Jesus took place, in spite of being an exotic and even – maybe – black; she foreshadows those other wise men from far away who were led by their oriental, stargazing skills to recognise that Jesus was the Messiah and the King of Kings. The magi, and their forerunner the Queen, an outsider like them, announce the peace of Christendom, the catholic boast of union, the mother church who clucks and gathers into her brood all manner of different and outcast peoples under one faith.

In the Koran too, and in later Muslim embellishments on her story, the Queen of Sheba wants to create peace. She understood the finesses required by diplomacy, and so she responded to Solomon's letter with blandishments and much praise of his reputation and heaps of presents, arguing with her courtiers that she hoped to hold him at bay with such means, but feared that if he were a true potentate, he would not give in at an early stage, but demand more. She wouldn't show enmity when he summoned her, but go to meet him, if they were in accord. They were; this was a womanly way of doing things, it has a long history – this is somewhere I come in – and even though she was the ruler of her country, she was expected to know it too, by instinct. Presently, as she anticipated, Solomon refused her gifts and summoned her in person.

She was aware of the dangers he posed for her and for her people in her absence; she garrisoned the capital and strengthened the border, and she concealed the national treasure, and its greatest jewel, her throne, in a deep cave behind seven doors, each of which she had locked with a combination code, to which seven different trusted colleagues, all unknown to one another, possessed the secret. But she kept back a single pearl – 'an unpierced pearl' – and shut it in a casket in her luggage to give to Solomon. If she felt like it. Or so the Muslim chroniclers say.

Then she loaded the caravan with gold and myrrh and oil and other produce of her southern country and chose a hundred Sheban children to follow in her train and see the land of Solomon and broaden their minds. But because she wanted them to return with her, and Solomon's appetite was famous, she proposed they should disguise themselves. Some of the fifty boys were to be dressed as girls, some of the fifty girls as boys, and she checked their appearance before the journey began, and satisfied herself that no one would be able to tell which was which.

The djinns, at their master's order, swarmed south, slipped the catch on the first lock, then on the second, then the third, and so forth, until they penetrated to the innermost chamber of the mountain hideaway, and shouldering the precious throne on their leathery bat-wings, they whisked it to Jerusalem, passing it from one to another until it was landed at Solomon's feet. The anomalous Queen was to learn who had mastery. Then Solomon issued another command, and the djinns again set to work pumping hard to bring the spring of Gihon from the valley of Kidron where it gushes up from the earth's mantle up through the underground tunnel that secretly connects the valley with the Temple. Once the jet spurted, Solomon ordered his demons to channel it into a stream flowing in front of his dais. They did so; he threw in crumbled biscuits to make sure fish were still present, and then, with a stern eye, froze the water hard as glass. The fish remained visible within it, trapped like ammonites in rock.

The security around the Temple, where Solomon expected the Queen's embassy, was tight. The hundred children in her train were taken aside separately and questioned; many of them had to identify their own baggage and order it down from the camels and open it under the eyes of Solomon's guards.

The Queen of Sheba fumed. She was kept waiting outside the Temple gates for the search of her entour-age to be completed. Beside her, Solomon's guards chattered; at least they did not submit her to the indignity of interrogation.

He wants to put me out of countenance, she told herself, I must not let him. He'll gain the advantage if I become agitated and cross. Just hold on, think of other things. The sky here, is it a different colour? The light here, is it brighter, harsher? The men here, is their build different? Will he be handsome? Strange how the guards are all bearded; in our country only old men wear hair on their face. Will Solomon have a beard too?

Her nostrils and lips twitched at the thought of the scratchiness. Again, she rebuked herself for her drift, and stirred impatiently on the rug they had spread for her wait. She followed the pattern in the weave of hawkmoth heads, hung in tiers as in a collector's vitrine. It's standard practice, she continued, there's been trouble, everybody who enters the Temple must be searched, a man once pulled a dagger on the King, and if one of his bodyguards hadn't flung himself between the assailant and the King in time and taken the force of the attack, the King would be dead. As it was, the blade passed clean through the guard and its tip grazed the King's side all the same, it was so sharp and so long.

Perhaps it would have been better if he had been killed, thought the Queen, flexing her hands, which were moist with the tension of her vigil. No, Solomon's successor might have been worse. Besides, she wanted to set eyes on him for herself, she'd been told so much about his power, his knowledge, his roomfuls of books and pictures from all over the world. She must keep calm: it was politics. A foreign power always displayed its muscle in front of the ruler of another, small, unknown neighbour, however grand a show she had put on to sue for peace as an equal. The Queen sighed. The spices and furs and gold and gems she had brought would have sustained Shebans for a long time; but she wanted to hide the poverty and difficulties suffered by her people: she knew men kick the dog that lies sickly in the street but pet the hound that leaps and races at the leash.

A guard picked out one of the young members of the Queen's train and lifted the curtain of a booth to usher her in. The Queen outside clasped her hands, and pressed her pulse down on her lap to steady her blood rate; she was afraid.

Inside, the young woman soldier bunched up her fists like a child miming stone in a game of Paper, Scissors, Stone and passed them over the Sheban's body with practised speed. She traced the outside outline of her body, down over her hips, up the inside leg to the crotch, and fanned out over the back, shoulders and chest like a tailor drawing with chalk on a toile to mark adjustments. Underneath the Sheban livery of grey and primrose-yellow pyjamas the boy's flesh shivered as the rough girl's hands caressed him, with shyness, with fear that she might become aware of his disguise, with pleasure. But the soldier's features remained expressionless, and when she said, 'You're clear,' she spoke dully, as she pulled back the curtain of the green booth and showed him out.

Then, 'No body search today, for you,' she added. 'You're in luck.' Was there an emphasis, a touch of humour? He couldn't tell, and he flounced the panels of his tunic coquettishly, to share the joke with her, if she'd understood. But she was already ushering in another. (Later the guards would giggle together in the mess about the day, the wriggling girls in the men's searches, the stiff shy boys in the women's. But they didn't tell, because they were looking principally for concealed knives or hammers and besides, they assumed the disguises were part of the visiting barbarians' outlandish customs.)

The Queen relaxed as she saw the children regroup undetained, and enjoyed the success of her ruse. Solomon was insatiable, she'd heard. What did that mean? He had several hundred wives, and more women besides, it was said. How often could he do it? Again, she tried to check her line of thought. He's an adversary, a danger, you must use all your powers to keep him sweet. Yet, she thought again, how often can he get round all of them? She imagined the one chosen rising from a gaggle of recumbent houris, tense, pleased, smoothing her dress, no, adjusting her hair, perhaps she doesn't wear any dress. The Queen shook herself, rapped herself over the knuckles, surveyed the bustling gates. One of the children waved to her, laughing. The time came for her to make her approach. Apprehension was clamped to her gut, and gnawing.

She reminded herself, He is wise, they say, perhaps his wisdom will make him kind. The lines of attendants formed behind her, and, with a tap and a click, the baggage train began to move, the Queen of Sheba and her train entered the enclave of the Temple.

Solomon was sitting on a throne, and he did have a beard; he was smaller than she had expected, slighter in build, and he looked eagerly at her, as if he truly wanted to meet her. (*My beloved is white and ruddy, the chiefest among ten thousand. Saw ye him whom my soul loveth? His head is as the most fine gold . . .*) Her hopes rose, she stretched her step and approached. (*Rise up, my love, my fair one, and come away. For, lo, the winter is past, the rain is over and gone . . .*) She was trembling.

Points of light were darting from the jewels set in his throne, from the eyes of the lions couchant on each of the twelve steps, and bouncing in the sunlight off the water running across the courtyard before his dais. She was bewildered, she wanted to shade her eyes, but formality prevented her and besides she would need to hold up her dress to save it from getting wet. She mustn't show fear, she told herself, she mustn't hesitate, but go forward, answer his beckoning hand, his open, smiling glance. Then she saw her own throne, beside the dais, winking with its own constellation of starry stones, and their dancing lights mixed with the shooting flashes from Solomon's dais and the glints sparkling in the water in front of her, and the combined dazzle blinded her. She was unutterably dismayed. But she kept on, answering his greeting, and stepped out of her shoes as there was no bridge and this must be a custom in King Solomon's kingdom, and went towards him, into the water.

The school of fish beneath don't flick away from her in a flash of scales; they hang there, stock still; the water doesn't open to her advance. Solomon's eyes meet her confusion. He looks down, she feels his look lick her limbs. She follows the King's eyes and she sees that she is walking on mirror, her white petticoat's ruffle looks back at her, she can see her bare legs, and so can Solomon.

Are they monstrous? Are they hairy?

The Muslim storytellers differ.

In one tale, the djinns fix the Queen's problem in a jiffy, inventing a depilatory cream on the spot.

But that is a late, bastardised version – obviously by some comedian from the bazaar.

Is she hooved?

Maybe.

In other stories, the ones we know better, the Queen is beautiful all over. (*Thou art all fair, my love; there is no spot in thee.*)

Solomon chuckled. The success of his trick was splendid. He felt warmly towards the stranger Queen who had so compliantly fallen in with his plans; then a chivalrous pity filled his breast as he saw her discomfiture, her pain. He rose and came towards her, and they embraced as visiting heads of state, right hands clasped, heads bowed in respect, and in answer, she dropped a curtsy. Close to him, she could smell him, a slightly peppery, bitter smell, sweat in the gold gimp of his robes, ineradicable even by the dry-cleaning solvents of the wisest man in the world. He was not as young as he looked from below, but his lips were full, the upper one protruding ripely over the bottom as if ready to be kissed. (*His mouth is most sweet: yea, he is altogether lovely.*)

She was there to calm him down, to deflect his intentions on her country, to propose a treaty, to make friends. She must flatter him, she knew how much men like women to admire them; but she also understood that her flattery would mean nothing if she seemed too easy. Already she had been outwitted, already he had stolen an advantage.

The Queen rose from her curtsy and turned to ask for her shoes; one of her attendants knelt to dry her feet and she slipped them on.

She looked up and forced a smile; Solomon grinned back. 'I've a great many questions to put to you,' she said, 'for I've heard that nothing's hidden from your wisdom.'

The King waved his hands in modest dissent, but then nodded to tell her to proceed.

She showed him two identical roses. She told him that one was a true rose, and the other only cast in silver by the lost wax process so that every vein and speckle and delicate rib and curl of the petals and leaves of a rose was faithfully reproduced and then painted. She asked him how to tell the replica from the real thing.

Solomon considered the roses. Then he clapped his hands and gave an order to a djinn. The servant flitted away through the air, and returned with a hive, buzzing with bees; another ran up with a napkin; when he uncovered it, a donkey's mess inside, flyblown and steaming, released its fetor.

Solomon said to the Queen of Sheba, 'Watch.'

The flies buzzed around, tried the roses one by one and flew back to the dung; the bees circled, rose, and then one tacked in mid-air, reversed and flew down to the rose in her left hand, and bending its abdomen voluptuously to rub the gold dust on the stamens with its tail tip, nuzzled at the honey in the centre of the flower.

'You see,' said Solomon, 'bees can tell the counterfeit.'

Though she had to drop the rose to avoid the bees, the Queen was impressed, and pleased to see that Solomon seemed to appreciate her test. 'We're too much slaves of the eye altogether,' she said. 'Touch and smell and taste and hearing – these other means of understanding are far too easily overlooked, don't you think, O King?'

And Solomon, amused by the barbarian Queen's earnestness, nodded, in complete agreement. (That is the riddle she posed and the fable as told, and if it seems to connect with what I tried to say that night with the boys, then it's none of my doing.)

She tried him again, with another question, dear to her and more so to me. She was ticking off the number of her riddles on her fingers, schoolmistressy, not to be put off.

'Boys and girls are different in their bodies, I know,' she said, 'but are they different in their minds?'

The stories we have are bent on covering Solomon in glory, and so, immediately, effortlessly, brilliantly, he naturally finds an answer.

Again he whispered a command to a servile djinn and again, when the djinn returned he was carrying something, in a bulging net sack, which he hoisted over to the King, who, shouting to the Queen's train of youths, dipped into it and chucked with boisterous, Santa-like cheeriness a succession of brightly coloured balls, a cascade of sweets and toffees and chocolates and gobstoppers and liquorice shoelaces and allsorts and lollipops and humbugs, into the group of girls and boys, of boys dressed as girls and girls dressed as boys. One after another his gifts tumbled pell-mell into the company.

The Queen looked on while her servants caught Solomon's scattered largesse, and saw nothing but a mêlée. But Solomon crowed.

'I knew it, I knew it,' he whooped. 'The boys jump for what they want, they snatch, they scrap, they go for it – even if you have togged some of them up like houris, while the girls, well, I'm glad to see that even from your country they're proper little women, aren't they, and thank God for it. They're making their choice carefully, aren't they, gathering up the sweets one by one from the ground, and putting them in their skirts and if they aren't wearing skirts because for some reason you've got them done up as sentries then they're filling a corner of their tunics with the stuff as if in an apron. You thought you could take me in, but you can't!' He was pink with delight at his success, he was almost breaking into applause, his laughter was making his eyes glisten, when he noticed that the Queen was still standing.

'Come now,' he said, taking her gently by the waist, 'Kneeling shows the female sex, as your little ladies have shown us, but you, you gorgeous thing you, you must be seated.' And he handed her to her own throne. (*He brought me to the banqueting house, and his banner over me was love . . . His left hand is under my head, and his right hand doth embrace me.*)

She was shaking. She had heard that in other countries like Solomon's women were kept in seclusion as the possessions of their husbands, but she had not experienced the custom at first hand. In Sheba, she knew about women's weakness too, but there, differences between women and men did not mean that one sex ruled or laughed or mocked the other; besides she was disillusioned that he was so literal in his answer, that he proposed such a basic solution to the conundrum she had posed.

But he laughed at her commotion; and with a conjuror's flourish, produced from his sleeve that unpierced pearl she had brought in her tribute and concealed in a casket. He began tracing a spider's web in the air, wafted it, caught a thread from it, pulled it free, and passed it through the pearl to hang it round his neck.

At least this is how I imagine the encounter with Solomon took shape, this is how I see her, waking up to the idea that it's hard for a woman to make her own conditions and impose them if she has to live alongside men. They throw her coloured balls, they throw her sweets, and she kneels to pick them up, like me. She keeps something for herself, something secret and precious, but they conjure it out of the air; they sport it as trophies and laugh at her dismay.

In Ethiopia – and according to many authorities, Sheba lay there, in the Horn of Africa – Solomon marries the Queen and she has a child – they call him Menelek – with him, with whom she returns to Sheba. She raises him to become the first of the Lions of Judah, direct ancestor of the Emperor Haile Selassie and founding father of the Rastafarian cultists today, in their tricolour bonnets over felted cigarillo dreadlocks.

In the chapel of the Ethiopians in Jerusalem, on the whitewashed roof of the church of the Holy Sepulchre, past the beehive cells of the few sable-hued monks who remain, the Queen of Sheba's meeting with Solomon and their ensuing love fill the panels of a painting along one wall. Scarlet, saffron, viridian figures, huge-eyed as nocturnal mammals, move through the frames of a devotional strip cartoon to tell of her magnificent and exalted capitulation to the wisest man in the world, and of the peace she brought to Sheba by her alliance, when she became Solomon's beloved (*my sister, my spouse*), and converted to his faith and thus founded Ethiopian Christianity.

Idyll of Africa, gentle southern parable concealing an ancient surrender: its ending didn't always turn out so sanguine. In Yiddish folklore, the Queen of Sheba metamorphoses into Lilith, demon woman, bloodsucker, child murderer, the woman who defied Adam's authority from the very start, in Eden, just as the Queen of Sheba, in her unattached state, threatened the code by which polygamous Solomon and his patriarchal descendants live. In this cycle of stories, the Queen returns to Sheba as she came, unmarried, with her store of arcane knowledge, an unseemly thing in woman. She remains childless herself, even hating all children; amulets were made to prevent her preying on babies in their cradles.

But in the median version, the favourite among Muslim storytellers, the Queen of Sheba receives her trouncing at the hands of the wise King, as is only right, converts to his God – in this case, Allah – and accepts his laws, including the custom, unfamiliar in Sheba, of marriage. Solomon chooses her a husband, and gives her several of his djinns to slave for the pair of them and set them up in their new household. The djinns are tremendously relieved that Solomon does not marry her himself, for the offspring of such a union would inherit redoubled powers of sorcery and continue to hold them in subjection; with this lesser union, the djinns will be free when Solomon dies, like Ariel when Prospero breaks his wand. And indeed, as soon as they hear the news of the King's death, years after the Queen's embassy, down tools they do, and refuse to work for her or her husband ever again.

I was standing on the ramparts of the Old City of Jerusalem, looking across the valley of Kidron, with George H., a most knowledgeable guide and friend – he was born in Jerusalem, in the Armenian quarter. After my paper to the conference that morning, I'd given the others the slip. I didn't much want to face them, after my small but painful collusion and betrayals.

George was pointing towards a shallow hill opposite, its shield-shaped crown densely fringed by dark green trees, as if it were wearing a cap pulled down on its head. And in the boneyard barrenness of the Judaean terrain, the mere sight of such woody shade is refreshing as a glass of water.

'That's where Solomon kept his women, or so the story goes,' George told me. 'He had to make sure of them, so he kept them at a distance from the city, in a high place, with guards set around.' The disapproval of George, who is a mystic of determined Christian persuasion, sounded clearly in his voice.

(*But King Solomon loved many strange women . . . he had seven hundred wives, princesses, and three hundred concubines . . .*) There was henbane bristling at the wall as we looked towards the hill, the hill of Silwan. It had opened its yellow face and purple throat to the passing bees; if the Queen of Sheba had had freckles, she might have decocted the leaves to bleach them.

'I'd like to go there,' I said. We took a taxi up the hill into the wood; there was long damp grass under the pine trees, and golden aconites were in flower, wearing lacy ruffs like the subjects of Dutch portraits, and small wild blue iris pulled leopard-spotted tongues and cyclamen uncurled in the moist shadows with their pink ears folded back and cryptograms printed on their dark emerald hoof-shaped leaves. Lemon trees were flowering and fruiting at once, and there was a scent of fresh sweetness in under them. Here perhaps Solomon and the Queen exchanged love songs once. (*Thy navel is like a round goblet . . . Thy two breasts are like two young roes that are twins, which feed among the lilies.*)

The hill commanded a sweep over the city: the excavations of the City of David, child of Solomon by one of his wives, were laid out in fretwork under the stacked bleached stone of Jerusalem; Absolom, David's son, was buried under the dagoba-style monolith hewn from the valley floor and face below; on the other side, the mirror of the Dead Sea, mercury and milk and mother of pearl, shone beyond the frozen ocean of the dunes' rise and fall in the desert.

This is where she opened to her beloved, when she put her hand in at the door and felt her fingers drip with myrrh and her insides turn over for him. (*Honey and milk are under thy tongue.*) And even though I had to disapprove – I wanted her not to concede anything, let alone that unpierced pearl, I wanted her to emerge untouched – I couldn't help feeling pleasure too in the fragrant wood with the valley of Kidron below where the water of Gihon still wells up.

The door of the building that now stands on the hill in the wood of Silwan opened in its turn, and a gaunt woman in the grey habit of a nurse hurried down the steps towards us. She was fluttering; there had been a few foreigners murdered recently in Jerusalem, by terrorists of as yet unidentified affiliation, and she was nervous of strangers, it was plain. George explained, 'We are researching the traditions about King Solomon; she –' he pointed at me – 'is a visitor from England, a teacher.' The nurse relaxed. Her face was waxy from washing it in water, her posture bent, ingratiating, and she had a gold incisor, which gleamed, and an enamel badge of the Virgin Mary at her throat. She answered, 'Yes, there is a story, but I don't know much about it. That Solomon kept his . . . I don't know the word.' And she twittered.

George, who speaks most languages, supplied it.

'His harem, yes, that's it,' she said. She repeated the phrase and peered around short-sightedly. I followed her look; of course it was fixed on nothing but the pines.

There were sounds, though, and scents; above all a song. (*Make haste, my beloved, and be thou like to a roe or to a young hart upon the mountains of spices.*) I wanted not to hear. Fight back, I said to myself. Resist the longing. Ass's hooves are fine. Hairy legs are fine. Don't let yourself hear the song. And don't listen, when you do.

III
FATHERS & DAUGHTERS

In the Scheme of Things

F ive years of catastrophes, but the ruler had held the nation together. He wasn't to blame, not for the visitations of fate on his country; not even he could have the power to descry the writing of destiny before it appeared on the wall. Only a despot of the old school would presume to know the mind of the Almighty and employ priests to read signs, in knuckle-bones or shoulderblades or the entrails of animals. His was a modern régime, and its ruler understood man's place in the scheme of things, as did his people. They didn't expect him to conjure order from chaos, to set against the dealings of fortune the petty strength of the human hand. But they were grateful, very grateful, for his providence and understanding. Without him, the condition of the people would be far worse. No, they didn't blame him, they didn't blame him at all.

The disasters had been untoward, it had to be admitted. No one had ever heard of such plagues before, in such quick succession, at least not since Yahweh blasted the Egyptians – as the rabbis were quick to point out. Spice merchants and ironmongers and green-grocers in the Jewish section of the covered market of his principal city pointed the finger at him, their ruler, he knew it, much more readily than other sections of his community, who loved him. They saw a connection between the chain of catastrophes and his dispensation. They called him, Pharaoh.

The ruler ground his teeth and bunched his fist at the thought, and decided he would command the palace chef to stop buying from them, even though Estella, his daughter, liked the almond biscuits they baked and their cheese blintzes and black cherry soup and home-made paprika dumplings more than anything in the world, or so she said.

Looking back, he supposed that the catastrophes had begun in his first year of office, when the Library in the main square caught fire one night and the conflagration spread through Foreign Literature in Translation, Social & Political Science, and had begun to consume History before the firemen got the blaze under control. He visited the scene the next day, and made a public statement of mourning for the lost collection, for centuries' worth of knowledge destroyed. His nose was still filled with the sharp scent of burned books. Curious, he had thought, it was almost an organic smell, almost fragrant, like roasting meat.

The ruler had directed the public inquiry to search among the literary community. It was bound to be one of them who'd set the fires, he told the tribunal in confidence. Writers were an unstable, envious lot. And even if you kept them corralled into writers' colonies, as he tried to do, giving them every opportunity and privilege of practising their craft securely, you couldn't be sure you'd caught every one.

But the police hadn't come up with a guilty party, unfortunately, though they'd detained a strong suspect for a while, and nearly achieved a confession. A novelist. The ruler sighed, and wrote a memo to himself to ask the Chief of Police about the last writers' tally. He hoped the number of writers was decreasing. Or else he might have to take further action.

After the Library fire, the next disaster had been – he pondered a while, it was easy to confuse the chronology – yes, that was it, another fire, this time in the shafts bringing the mint workers up from the bullion vaults. That was a strange case: thirty-five dead and several others so badly burned they would have to wear surgical masks until the skin grafts could be done. And there was a waiting list for the surgeons who had the skills required for such delicate work. It seemed someone had chucked out a cigarette on stepping into the lift, and the litter at the bottom of the shaft had caught alight. Only a bonfire, really, but it had burned through the cable and brought the cage crashing down. Then the rescue work – well, it turned out that the emergency stairs hadn't been used for a while, and the maintenance had been neglected . . . The ruler dismissed the thought – it was too distressing to him, and to no purpose.

Think of the natural disasters instead, he admonished himself. Look on the bright side, as his mother used to tell him. Turn your mind to the calamities for which nobody could possibly be responsible: don't think of the shipwreck, when the boat slewed round, filling with water at its rear end until it pitched over and plunged the passengers into the winter sea. Don't consider the airbus that lost a wing over the chief city of the inner plain, or the street sliced through by the giant torn-off limb as it careened down to earth followed by the broken fuselage. Or the small plane that exploded . . . or the trains that collided and in the impact passed clean over one another, like coupling rhinos. No, he scolded himself, a gloomy outlook will not do. He had always held to a strictly materialist view, according to the principles of his upbringing. But these days, he began to feel stirrings of sympathy with those growing numbers among his subjects who believed in a dangerous malign force at work. Perhaps after all, someone was to blame, someone busy undermining the central power, his own righteous authority. There were some among his people who were becoming impatient with his scepticism, who clamoured that divine vengeance was behind the disasters, and would increase in vigour until it was recognised and given due worship. Some religious groups demanded public expiation, urging their ruler to recognise the close battle joined on earth between the powers of darkness and of light. He should rise and combat the powers of evil, he should root out the wicked.

He wouldn't have paid attention to them in old, secular times, but he had to watch the direction of the wind if he were to fulfil his promise as a good ruler.

The faithful were prone to point a finger here, another there. Who knows who they might finger next. The ruler grasped his pen and began writing a memo to the Chief of Police. He must have these new fanatics watched, before they overtook him in his plans. Perhaps there was a grain of truth in what they said, that God has His own ways; that there's a hidden meaning to His plans. He sends trials to test us.

Like the sudden plague of leeches: it had become difficult, in his kingdom, to go for a walk without finding one or more of the creatures fastened to one's flesh, burrowing in at both ends, it seemed, liquid patent leather curls squirming for a good grasp. They'd been known in the country for a while, of course, and country people knew to look out for them, examine themselves carefully coming in from the outdoors, in the creases and folds of flesh – small children were especially vulnerable – but since last year the problem had arrived in the cities.

And now there was this flower that had sprung up among the crops, a beautiful thing, Asiatic witchweed, the botanists called it, with a translucent purple corolla and scarlet stamens. It could reduce a crop to chaff within a week, leaving fields luxuriantly ablaze with colour and no harvest. He had called his agricultural physicists to analyse the prodigy immediately. They had reported back that the flower had no root: that it blew through the air and plugged itself into whatever host it could find, corn or barley or oats, whatever, and that it could simply adapt itself to suit. It was like the best of guests, at home anywhere, in any company, at any function; and they could think of nothing to stop its continuing triumphant conquest of their society's food supply.

So when the salamanders were washed up on the beach down by the coastguard station, most witnesses were relieved they were dead. That they weren't capable of breeding any more, of infesting the countryside and the cities and duplicating themselves with green scaly progeny. They lay on the shingle, their scalloped ruffs closed like broken umbrellas, their iridescent scales dull and rimed with salt, their tails loose as wrack on the highwater mark; they looked like so many dragons eviscerated by Saint George. Though the stench was overpowering, the people swarmed down to the water's edge to look at them; some poked with a foot at the heap of dead reptiles, others stood, holding their noses, and kept their distance. A man kicked over a head, to look into the pale green snout of the salamander, and its veined eyelids, lying over sunken eyeballs, were as translucent as new beech leaves in summer. Another poked at the carcass of a big brute, and as its foreleg, crowned with claws, rose up under the prodding boot and fell back, a shudder ran through the crowd.

Then there was a stir in the jetsam, the flick of a tail on the shingle and one beast raised his head from among his drowned companions and swung it slowly from side to side, pulling one leg from the tangled bodies, then another, as he lifted himself upright again.

Some people in the crowd shrieked; the children cringed into the shelter of the nearest adult, but thrilled, breathless with anticipation, clinging on in order to prevent the retreat up the beach that had begun. But when the salamander first opened his dark mouth, the spectators couldn't be restrained, certainly not by children. At the sight of the long, slender, black tongue whipping from side to side, like a line played by a fly-fisherman in a trout stream, a howl went up. The crowd broke up, some scrambled back to the promenade above the beach, mobbing the narrow steps; they were screaming when they could not make headway, and they squeezed up so tight that the older people present were carried by the momentum of the crush and would have been trampled if they had fallen. Others rushed the animal, as he lumbered up the shingle towards them, and then fanned out around him, shouting to head him off.

'The brute's coming this way!'

'Drive it back!'

'Hold it down!'

'Don't let it past!'

'This way!'

Some yarrupped and clicked at the beast, as he stepped clumsily one way then the other in confusion.

'Into the sea – drown the monster!'

The salamander was still dazed from his passage in the cold ocean and the exposure to horror he had endured: he had known nothing like it in his earlier existence, not even in the cramped ship's cistern let

alone the baked desert, where he had been captured
originally by a specimen hunter for sale to a luxury pet
shop. Faced with the jeering, menacing ring of men
and women who were picking up stones and throwing
them at him, forcing him back into the horrible cold
ocean he had so miraculously survived, the beast summoned up all his powers: he stood fast beneath the
assault, the pebbles falling harmlessly off his green
scales which were beginning to glow again with defiant
rage. As he stood there taking their blows, the people
saw his tail stiffen with muscle, its forked end spark
with fire where it lashed the beach, his frilled wings
spread like a swan's, his neck arch and his emerald ruff
rise in points to make an aureole around his head; now
the tongue darted back and forth among the flames
that flickered in the air before him. Though he had
inflated his size to full fighting panoply, he was still
much smaller than his assailants.

The stoners faltered. The impression the beast made
was of a much bigger creature, and one growing more
huge by the minute. Some held back through fear;
others began to cry out in wonder. At the back a child
was wailing, 'They're going to kill it. They're going to
kill it,' over and over.

Then one of the most enthusiastic stoners dropped
his arm and shouted, 'Take it to the Ruler! Let him
decide!'

Others took up the cry, dropped their missiles and
began making gurgles of encouragement, clucking and
trilling and snapping their fingers to bring the animal

to heel like a pup. But he continued to stand his ground, unmoved, swaying his long neck and flicking the black cord of his tongue into the flames hissing from his jaws and nostrils, until the police arrived with a net of a fine metal wire and threw it over him and pulled the drawstring tight and then dragged him up the ramp used for launching the lifeboat (in the days when there had been a lifeboat and volunteers to crew it) and left him on the boardwalk above the beach, near the bandstand, until the ruler could come and decide his fate.

Estella was with her father when the news of the Beast's coming and its miraculous survival was brought to the palace.

'It's an omen, Daddy, an evil omen,' she said, plaintively. 'Another one.'

'We don't believe in omens, darling.' But to his daughter, his tone was indulgent. 'We leave that to the superstitious, to people of little brain, who find significance in everything and fear it.'

He wanted her to come with him, but she wouldn't. Estella did not add that she had a feeling about the beast, that it was destined for her, that something out of the sea was seeking her out, specially, and she was scared. He cajoled her, and when she still resisted, he made her. He could not have his only child as scared as an ignorant peasant before random, meaningless prodigies.

The police chief had ordered the disposal of the

corpses on the tideline; the reptiles were being burned on the shore and the reek was appalling, a smell of tyres and rotten meat together.

As they approached the trapped animal, they could hear howling through the hissing of his flaming breath, and, as they stood by, they watched him flail in the net. The princess covered her face with her sleeve. Her father then gave the order, 'Bring the brute to the palace. Alive.'

As he turned away, the police, wearing riot gear, positioned themselves round the thrashing animal before they closed in.

'I want you to have it, my darling, as a present,' the ruler said when the salamander was brought to the palace. 'It'll make a pet fit for a queen!' He thought it very funny when his daughter turned pale at the gift.

The salamander's jaws were muzzled and his claws had been clipped by the police surgeon. 'It'll make a splendid guard dog, you'll see. The fire-eating'll stop, as soon as it's used to its new surroundings. It'll learn which side its bread is buttered soon enough!' And the ruler roared with laughter.

When her father laughed, there was no point arguing. Estella took the leash the police officer handed to her, and murmured something by way of thanks.

'What's that you say?' he shouted, and slapped his thigh with delight as she led the beast off to her quarters. 'She'll soon see. Nothing can scare me, nor the flesh of my flesh. She'll learn. Nothing.'

For some time, Estella couldn't bring herself to look

at the beast. She remembered an old aquarium in which she'd once kept some tropical fish and she allowed a light to burn above it to keep the creature warm, after one of her maids told her that salamanders needed heat. She called the girl in, since she seemed to have a way with animals, when the beast needed to have its muzzle off to eat and drink. But she couldn't bear to hear it feed, prolonging its hateful life. She wanted to wake up one morning and find the salamander dead.

One afternoon, as the sun moved round with the lengthening days, the beam reached the tank where the salamander was confined, and she found herself watching it bask. The green scales glowed in the light, flecks glancing off their scalloped edges. She became curious; she approached the small dragon-like creature in her keeping and put out her hand to the flames in its breath. She found that its fire was pleasant to the touch, like a warmed stone. She tried again, reached out farther and a flame curled around her fingers, sending shivers of pleasure through her. The black tongue followed, wrapped itself around her wrist and lit her up, a quick rush of white heat shooting up her arm and suffusing her all over. She cried out, softly, and reached to fondle the creature's head. Again the flames flushed her with pleasure and the tongue's movement made her tingle. She reached into the fish tank and picked up the salamander and gently set it down.

'Let's go for a walk,' he said. 'I need some fresh air.'

They walked. Now she found something magnificent in his step, in the green fan of his ruff and the

heavy somnolence of his long neck and tail. She skip-
ped to keep up with him, feeling like a little girl beside
him, being shown the world for the first time.

On that day, and day after day after that, for as long
as happiness was allowed them, they explored, first the
palace gardens, then the country beyond. She walked
in the chief city of her father's realm for the first time
without ceremonial attendants. She spoke to strangers.

Together, they found secret places where they could
lie down. In an orchard one day, they curled together
under the apple tree and the blossoms fell on them like
confetti. She couldn't believe that she had once found
him ugly, or that she had feared him. His body was
more beautiful to her now than anything she had
known, and the touch of his breath on her skin made
her quiver inside.

Their conversations were long, intense, filled with
anxieties and punctuated with laughter. Sometimes
they quarrelled: the privileges that she had always
enjoyed occasionally made her touchy, when she saw
he was horrified by her ignorance. Sometimes, the
pleasure that they could give each other made them
want to test their powers of resistance and the bound-
aries of their dominion over each other. She came to
trust him, and with that trust she discovered many
things about herself and her feelings she had not been
able to voice before. She saw now how people were
suffering under her father. How many hundreds of
people had mysteriously disappeared, her own mother
among them. How the accidents that had befallen the

kingdom weren't meaningless, as her father the ruler always maintained.

'Be careful, my love,' said the beast, when she confided in him her new, disturbing thoughts.

'But there is such a thing as responsibility,' she cried. 'Fate can't be blamed for everything.'

Estella couldn't altogether believe that her father was blind to the discoveries she had made.

'I was thinking, Daddy,' she said, as they were talking together one evening, after dinner. 'Couldn't we declare a national day of mourning, for my mother and for all the others who've disappeared who knows where? Like armistice day, when everyone could wear flowers in commemoration of the fallen. White violets – they were her favourite flower, I remember.'

The ruler was eating a peach. It stuck in his craw. When he'd stopped choking, he asked Estella, 'Who's been putting such ideas in your pretty little head?'

'I can think for myself, you know,' she said. 'I'm growing up.'

Another evening, she suggested, 'You know the inquiry into the Library burning? Don't you think it should be reopened? I mean, it is terrible we lost all those books, and really, Daddy, no stone should be left unturned, don't you think?' In her teens, she was acquiring a rather imperious manner, like a princess in a fairytale.

Her father had her maids questioned. No, she wasn't meeting anybody, she wasn't seeing anyone. She spent all her days with the salamander, wandering in the gardens. She was never out of their sight, they assured him. Nobody who attended her had ever seen her so rosy, so alert, so eager to begin the day and so fulfilled at its close. She slept easy, and her dreams were sweet. No, she wasn't at all frightened of the beast any more, they informed the ruler. She could even place her hand in its fire.

Her father decided to have her tailed.

The spy reported back that his daughter and the beast had picnicked together by the trout stream at the foot of the chase beyond the chestnut drive, on a salad of radishes, tomatoes and baby carrots they had picked themselves on the way.

'I don't want to hear the menu!' roared the ruler.

'The subjects then went swimming together,' the spy stumbled on. 'The young woman took off her dress and frolicked in the water until the salamander joined her.'

'Frolicked?' roared the ruler, again, lunging for the spy's throat.

'She wasn't naked,' he spluttered. 'She kept her petticoat on.'

'Petticoat?' The ruler threw the spy on to the floor and kicked him in the groin.

Then he gave the order for the arrest of the salamander.

That evening he summoned the palace spokesman and issued a statement.

'Since the unforeseeable arrival of the monstrous salamander on our shores, the number of catastrophes that have befallen our beloved people has increased apace. In view of this distressing and intolerable chain of events, and in reparation to the dead and the many victims afflicted in divers ways, it is hereby decided to bring the culprit to book. No longer shall we in our benevolence point to the hand of Fate: the mercy which we have shown before has been exhausted by the foul malice of the beast who has come among us. The monster is hereby charged with sedition against our state, for which the only penalty is death.'

In private, the ruler told the press that he repented of his earlier scepticism. His daughter had been right to fear the creature; she – and the many God-fearing subjects in his kingdom – had shown greater wisdom than their loving ruler when they discerned divine judgment in the tragic events that had overtaken them. He begged forgiveness for his error, which had only risen from his desire never to suspect or see evil in others, but only good. Now, he realised, the devil was at work in his beloved country, and the salamander was his servant. With him exterminated, the nation and its people's woes would be at an end.

'He was a malignant omen,' said the ruler to his weeping daughter. 'You were quite right, my dear. Since he appeared, there's been nothing but trouble.'

'Half the things happened before ever he . . .' But Estella faltered when she saw the rage in her father's face. 'You know that,' she went on, under her breath.

She sat in court to hear the trial. Without the caresses of the beast's tongue on her flesh, she could not talk to him, nor he to her. Language between them had been altogether private, had enclosed their world and made it for each other alone. She stopped crying when she realised how bereft she was; all that was left inside her felt like a shaft of ice, frozen solid.

The trial was over rather quickly, given the silence of the defendant and the terror of the defence counsel who had been appointed to observe due process of law. The salamander was sentenced to be burned to death for the murder of thirty-five persons in the bullion vaults, the destruction of the Library, the crash of the airbus, and the plague of Asiatic witchweed.

Estella, on the day of his death, took a handful of apricots in a scarf of shot-green silk he had liked her to wear, a toothbrush and a change of underwear, and left the palace.

One of her maids heard her, but was loyal and did not give the alarm. When Estella reached the boundary fence she crawled under it, at the place that she and the salamander had dug together and kept concealed with brushwood. On the other side she stood a moment and spat on the ground, a curse on her father, and a curse on herself, too, for not running away with the salamander long before, when they were still safe in their secret.

The salamander was bound at the stake, like all traitors; but he did not burn. He lashed out, flames leaping from his jaws, until the exasperated ruler gave the order for the executioner to spear him through the heart. When the flames had died down, the beast was flayed and the flashing green trophy of his scaly skin displayed on a post in the main square. The faithful gazed on it in awe, and many sighed and gave thanks that the devil's henchman had been stopped in his evil-doing. They applauded the ruler who, in his ineffable wisdom, had identified the author of their problem and rooted him out.

Long afterwards, when the ruler had been deposed, the government of the invaders bequeathed the salamander skin to the new Museum of Atrocities they had inaugurated. It was prominently displayed, next to a charred book, a testimony, the label said, to the bygone ruler's attempt on History. The skin was still sulphurously green, and a pearly light played along the edges of the scales as vivid as in the creature's lifetime. Estella was in her early forties when she returned home – under a different name. She went to visit the mortal remnants of her dear friend once or twice, though she didn't need to look on his hide to remember their love. She didn't mourn; she knew he hadn't been the sort to want her to dwell on the past.

Full Fathom Five

And the rain was upon the earth forty days
and forty nights. In the selfsame day entered
Noah, and Shem, and Ham, and Japheth, the
sons of Noah, and Noah's wife, and the three
wives of his sons with them, into the ark . . .

Genesis 7: 12–13

Father – for so I'm told I must call him – gave us
the bunk in the middle of the boat, the 'bridal
suite', though it was hardly as wide as a single
bed, and really a part of the corridor. That's not what
it's called – is it 'companionway'? No, that's the stairs. I
can't remember now what the right word is. Anyhow.
There was a curtain we could pull across if we wanted
privacy, Father said, with a heavy nudge, though I
wasn't meant to notice. Or show I'd noticed. That was
between the boys, between James and Father.

Actually, it so happens I can't bear to be overheard
in bed, and I can't enjoy myself much if I'm always
thinking I must keep quiet. Besides, I didn't feel much
like it at the time. Nor did James, to give him his due.

That first night, we couldn't sleep. The boat had looked so huge when it stood in Father's garden, hulking in its leggy cradle like a monster lobster. It embarrassed me, it made us look so . . . rich. But when the water swept us away the boat felt no sturdier than the brittle back of a leaf, and we spun in it like the twigs I used to break off to play poohsticks in the waterfall.

(The waterfall, the beautiful waterfall, which brought the flood.)

We used to watch while the stems bounced on the brown water, then went under the head of foam by the first reefs, then sometimes shot up again and sped over the falls down into the pool where the sheep came down to drink. Even in full spate, the stream below the waterfall was friendly, a laughing rill as they say, no broader than a jump anywhere, full of turns and spills. We used to dam it and divert it with the great grey loaves of slate it brought down from the mountain.

(You used to take me up there – to the moraine, as you called it – in the old days.)

The first night on board, our bunk was soaked through, and it never dried out again. The waves touched over our heads, like giants bowing to each other before a duel, and we'd skid around their skirts and just as they crashed together and fell in one huge breaker we'd somehow each time plane down the wall of water and escape, Father or one of the boys in a safety harness leaning on the wheel so they wouldn't be dashed overboard. I felt sick as a dog below, so I'd come up and tie myself to the rails until I couldn't take the sting of the sea on my cheeks any more and my nose could have been snapped off like an icicle. I couldn't ever get dry. We women gave up trying to keep ourselves dry, or anything else for that matter. James's mother hated it most of all, she wasn't used to wearing yesterday's shirts.

Perpetual greyness, perpetual rain. The men had two sets of oilskins between them, from Father's old yachting gear, and they took turns in them on deck. ('A lovely boat,' you used to say. 'Lovely lines.' Then, rolling your eyes to heaven, 'But for "weekend leisure sports", I ask you?' You envied Father.) 'The seams are bursting,' said James, when he came back from his watch, that first night. His eyes were scared. We lay there, and water spouted in our faces. It smelled rancid and its lash was full of grit. The boat tossed and shrieked, and though I desperately wanted comfort from him I was numbed inside as well as out and I couldn't move towards him or ask him or speak.

(We used to go up there, together. To the moraine, just you and I.)

You knew an awful lot about everything, it always seemed to me, even about stones and rocks and strata. The scenery up there was beautiful, in a kind of harsh, grand way, and you liked its bleakness. You were good at that, at seeing what there was to something. Good at telling stories about how things came about, about how things were to be.

The last time, before I was married, it was dry and

dusty, the wind lifted the black silt and filled our ears
and nostrils with light powder. I laughed at you, with
your miner's face and white clown's eyes behind your
glasses, and you responded in a bewildered way to my
laughter, looking at me short-sightedly, as you always
did when you provoked merriment in others though
you hadn't told a joke. I stopped laughing and I listened. You showed me the stain of the glacier's slow
heavy journey, higher up, and gathered pieces of rock
and loose pebbles and called them by their names –
mostly the slate from which we built our dams in the
stream below, but some of it feldspar, scintillating,
with purple flecks. You were worried, that last time,
that the glacier seemed to be on the move, so fast, all of
a sudden. Then you said you were an old man, and
your memory was playing tricks on you. You
chuckled, and added that it was impossible, the glacier
couldn't be flowing that fast, not unless some freak
conditions were at work. 'Wouldn't old Crane be
pleased if his catastrophic predictions are proved right?'
And you imitated the old anti-nuclear nuclear physi-
cist, screwing up your dusty lips and spitting out the
words in imitation of his reedy voice. 'Even if it does
mean Armageddon will carry him off as well as everyone else.'

I laughed, though I'd heard stories about this old
sparring partner of yours all my life, and most of them
more than once. I didn't give the glacier another
thought. But then the spring came, and with it the best
weather anyone alive had ever known. You suggested

a real dam be built, to contain the coming watershed. You spoke of hydroelectric power and new jobs in the region. I was impatient, all through May and June, whenever I was with you. I wanted to be with James, and you and James didn't get on, so I always went to see you alone. But it was never enough.

(If I had our time again together I'd be different, I swear.) You said that I never came to see you, and that when I did I wanted to get away again as fast as possible, that you were a foolish, fond old man, you knew, but since Violet – my mother – died you liked to see your daughter now and then. And I writhed and suddenly my tights would feel itchy and my T-shirt too hot – or too cold – and I'd try and tell you what I was up to, but as that revolved around James, he'd soon come into our conversation, and a malignant gleam would begin to cover your face, and you'd give a dry cough of a laugh and scorn the project, the enterprise, whatever James was up to. You could never forget the one time you visited the flat we'd taken together, when you gave vent to your spleen about our living together at all.

(Now I'd like to be able to go back to that time again. More than anything in the world, I want to have that time back.) You would certainly have said to me now, Too much of water hast thou, poor Ophelia. Whenever it rained and Mummy went out shopping and came in wet, that's what you'd say.

I can't remember ever feeling as sad as I did then. It was a sadness that was constantly interrupted by other feelings, by fear of the water swirling us God knows where, by the struggles to get the simplest task done, yet it never let me go even in the hell of the continual night, with the sky dark and close and cold as a wringing wet towel. Before the Flood, I used to luxuriate in grief, concentrating on it, growing it carefully, feeling it stretch my soul, making me deep and important. (*When something floated by and so much floated by, I saw you, I was scared, scared that it was you.*) I snapped at everyone, especially at James, and I knew it was because I couldn't fight with Father. He had me pinned down, like everyone else. Even the few animals we'd saved were meek with him, unruly with us. 'Pa is an autocrat,' James says proudly. I have to admit I was impressed by that too, when I first met James. That his father was who he was, the legendary magistrate, who could sit in judgment on two men in the same day for the same offence and sentence one to three years and let the other one clean off with a chuckle. 'If he likes the cut of your jib, that's the phrase,' James explained, 'he'll shout out from the bench, "I'm letting you off with a caution, this time," and then he'll bring down the gavel and bellow "Next", while the guy in the dock's ready to go out of his head with disbelief, the police having given him to know he'd be lucky to get away with his life.' I couldn't find it in me to admire him exactly, but I was impressed.

You looked down on him as a show-off and a loud-mouth, I know. Though you would have found better words, dictionary words.

(*When something floated by – and so much floated by – I*

kept on seeing you, I was scared it was you I was seeing.)
The bodies of women float by face upwards, staring
at the sky, they look like rag dolls with lidless eyes.
Sometimes their faces had lost their eyes, then they
were like old toys. Men's bodies float face down, as if
weeping. So I couldn't really have known if it was you
anyway. I remember when I was a little girl and getting
ready to go to school I used to come into the bathroom
to brush my teeth and often you'd be in the bath, white
and warm and lazy. I never saw you bask except those
times, when you'd lie in the tub, turning the hot tap
with your toes to top it up. In the garden, you'd never
lie on the lawn with us, but weed and move the hose,
even this last sweltering summer.

I wanted us to take you. I didn't want to leave you.
There wasn't room in the boat, Father said. You said I
should go – with my husband, my new family, you
said. 'Instead of some of the animals,' I pleaded, as
Father tossed a hutch on to the deck, 'Can't we take
him?'

It's your family now, you said. I shall be dead soon,
anyway, you said. Sooner or later, what's the difference?

The sun unlocked the glacier and it swept down over
the moraine. Your talk of dams was useless now. We
waited in the boat, on its spindly cradle, in Father's
garden, as the level began to rise. I had no idea then,
listening to the strained voice of the radio reporter,
how much I was going to mind leaving you behind.
'It's your duty, little woman,' you wrote to me just

before, using the words of childhood, 'to stay with your husband. The race must go on; the old be replaced by the new.' I could hear you sigh over your usual tag, 'Eheu fugaces, Postume, Postume.' You said you would wait, in the garden, that whatever measures the government might try to provide should not be used by the old. 'P.S.' you wrote. 'No mourning.' And underlined it three times. Then, in brackets: '(Should only be for the young.)'

I was safe in the boat, or as safe as anyone could be, with my husband and the father law has provided for me. All I could think of was sadness, how I let you down by joining them. I do mourn. I wouldn't have left you, then, when I was still separate from them, before my marriage. And I stuck to James in the first place partly to defy you, because you were so set against him and his family. In the same way as I took up smoking when you ordered me not to and blew out smoke in your face.

You'd been a teacher in a none-too-brilliant country school while Father had held sway over the imaginations of your charges. They called him 'Floggers', because he liked to joke that he regretted the disappearance of the cat-o'-nine-tails. They knew how he dealt with turbulent elements, how he could turn a youth who fancied himself a leader to a pale, yammering jellyfish of self-pity and cowardice in the dock. Ten years in the quarries for him, he'd hand down, while the police beamed. There were graffiti in your boys' toilets, you told me, warning, 'Floggers will get your balls', and 'Watch out, Floggers is watching you.' You despised all this, but you envied him all the same. One evening soon after James and I got married, we all arranged to meet for dinner in a restaurant, so the in-laws could get to know one another. Mummy was alive then and, I remember, she registered the strain long before it began telling on James and me. Her brown eyes, usually so pensive and slow in their rhythm, were darting over the menu, then scanning our faces as if something inside her had accelerated all her workings. There were no mishaps, no open conflicts. But when the time came to pay, Father took out his wallet and pulled a sheaf of notes and slapped it down on the bill. 'It's on me,' he said. 'But we invited you,' said James. 'Yes,' I said, 'It was our idea. We want to take you out.' 'Nonsense,' said Father, 'Since when has that rag you write for earned you an honest penny?' Then he wheeled his frame round square to you, and raised his strong red hand from the bill and jerked his jaw at it and said, 'Teaching doesn't pay, does it? But then, what would the country do without people like you?'

We were all turned into his creatures; he believed in the authority of his worldly success with such conviction that it leaked around him like gas, and at her end of the table, Mummy wilted.

I wish she hadn't died when she did, so that at least you could have sat together under the black sky waiting for the flood to come. Even though you argued, it would have been better to submit side by side.

I had to do the cooking on board, or at least take turns with the others. Miriam was having a baby and the smells from the galley made her feel sick; when she squatted over the side she looked sometimes as if she wanted to fall in and disappear. She'd lost her family too, we've talked about it often together since. So I took her shift. The boat pitched and heaved the stove about, even on the gimbals, and I banged into everything and it all seemed to be made of corners. We used to try and sit down, though the saloon – as Father made clear we must call it – was cramped for all of us. Leisure sports boats – even big family ones – aren't made for the Apocalypse; and the animals' stampede and yowling below as well as the ever-increasing reek made companionable eating ridiculous. But Father said we had 'to keep up our standards'; What were we made of, he boomed, if civilisation could be forgotten overnight? So I had to lay knives and forks and spoons and they clattered and banged and jumped off the table. One night – it was always night and there were no stars or moon to tell where we were or what time it was – I folded the omelette I'd made on to my portion of bread. Father exploded, 'And where were you brought up, young woman? In a sty?'

'You know where I was brought up,' I said. I thought, I wish I was there now.

'We're not in a sty here and don't you forget it.'

I clutched my sandwich with both hands and got up. 'I don't care,' I shouted. 'I don't give a fuck.'

'You take a hold on yourself, young woman,' he said, with his eyes hard and cheeks red.

I staggered up and swayed and made for the ladder and heaved myself up into the storming world, scattering bits of omelette and crumbs everywhere. For once I welcomed the sting of the salt sea on the wind.

James came, and looked helpless, and was sweet to me, though I knew it was because he wanted a peaceful life. Who could blame him? Also I was making his mother's position even more intolerable, with a tyrant on one hand and rebels on the other. I went down the ladder again, and swallowed all the witty things I'd thought of, and apologised. He told me we were all under a strain, that I was to keep making myself useful, and I wouldn't buckle. I had real reserves, he knew, 'underneath'.

So I went to fling out the muck from the animals' bedlam below, and even in the stench and roar of their terror, the cow's gently furred, blue-veined udders, her warmth and her silkiness were the greatest comfort I could have imagined. Her eye spun in a frenzied disc of bloodshot white as she tried to keep herself steady in the heaving and the pandemonium of the hold. I'd had no idea how to milk; none of us had. But I'd learned, and that night? that day? I felt the emptiness of the silky bag.

Father didn't like herbs in the food; I'd brought along my pots from our kitchen shelf, and though they turned yellowish in the constant darkness they were still scented and I liked to think they flavoured the tins of ham and pilchards we'd brought from the supermarket before the scare really cleaned out the shops. But when he saw the stray bits of leaf, he pushed his plate away. 'Fancy ideas about cooking, foreigners' fancies,' he said. 'Kind of thing your father encouraged.' And he waved at the blackness through the porthole as if the herbs and the tempest were one evil consequent on another. 'She's a very good cook, dear,' interposed the peacemaker, his wife. And I bit my protest back.

You had loved 'abroad' and he knew it.

It seemed for ever before the rainbow came. I was so wasted by then that I could hardly even smile at it, and when the sun burst from behind the tall chimneys of filthy grey cloud and exploded in ash-laden spokes, I blinked at the sudden light, like a nocturnal animal. James held me and squeezed me, with a kind of sensual pressure that we had never communicated for the whole stretch of eternity the boat had held us. He was quivering when he bent down and turned my face to his to kiss me.

'We'll be alone again,' he said. 'It'll be all right again.'

I felt the trembling seize me too, and I clutched tight, tight on his arm and kissed him back, babyishly dry sealed kisses like printing and felt my throat hot with the sobbing that doesn't make a sound, and thought, not yet. I can't be happy yet, not until you have been . . . and then I did not know quite what I wanted for you.

It was this: freedom to speak of you without constraint, to be proud of you. I needed to end the way you and I were kept apart, the way James's family inspired embarrassment and confusion in me on account of you and your difference from them.

Besides I needed revenge too, I suppose, though I didn't know how to get it.

James and I were doing up an old house that had stood the force of the flood. The roof had gone, but the walls were still solid and the site was beautiful, overlooking the new shore, towards the sunset, with the ruins of some town we did not know on the hill between. Father had moved into another house, further up the valley. The first summer after the flood was exceptionally fine, and everything was growing easily in the alluvial silt, a rich red-black, that the water had deposited in a layer one metre deep over everything. The fruit was sun-ripened to huge, glossy size; the vines' crabbed fingers held out grapes as big as plums. Just the smell of them when you squeezed one could give you a light head.

James and I were going over to Father's, as we often had to do – tools were in such short supply. We were walking through the new cornfield, when James heard something. A snuffle, a sigh, then a kind of a groan as a weight shifted.

Our survivors' talk was always of sightings – a footprint here, a distant, moving shadow there – but so far we had not met a single other human being.

James crept towards the snuffling. I followed him. Ahead of me, he went stiff, and seemed to fall back and want to turn and run, so I held him firm and looked round his shoulder. Under a tree, sprawled like the old winos we used to see under the bridge by the river before the Flood, with one arm flung out and his head thrown back, showing his mottled red gizzard above and the white tidemark where his collars covered his neck when they were buttoned up, Father was spread-eagled; he grunted and huffed through his open mouth, a little smirk playing in the corner of his stained lips. The other arm lay across him, and with his hand he had taken his cock out of his flies and was grasping it, like a pet rat in a pet-lover's hand peeping through the window of finger and thumb. James clapped his hand over my eyes, but I pushed his hand away, and I looked. Father pulled at himself blissfully. Then I began to laugh really loudly, and James tried to haul me away with him, and when I wouldn't come, he ran away. But for Father, it was too late; he opened one eye and swivelled it round till it landed on me and my laughter. At first a smile played lasciviously on his face, in answer. The response was fleeting, because then his other eye flew open, his hands came up and covered his face. He said, 'My God', scrambling, but still fuddled. I said, 'Oh, it's only you. We thought it might be someone new.'

I was glad for you, afterwards. Perhaps only for my idea of you. Father swore at James, but James didn't take it so badly. Father went ahead and cursed us, he said our children wouldn't be his blood, he disowned us, we weren't his family. But he couldn't pull rank on you or on me any more. He had been singled out all his life, privileged and beyond the reach of ordinary justice. But even death is not such a leveller as shame.

And I was glad, because I could then think of my child, who was born soon after, as belonging to our side only. I did what you told me, because you said I must. Stay with your husband, little woman, you have a new family now.

Heartland

————

The mark her father made to record a death was firmly drawn; it had been comparatively easy for him to cross clearly a strong downward stroke even when he could hardly see any more and the other characters formed by his hand had become indecipherable. Except to her. She was still the only person who could read Gus Lavery's last manuscripts. Occasionally she needed helpers, researchers, disciples, to fill in the allusions or uncover the references, themselves more cryptic sometimes than his writing, but there were students of her father's life who would flesh out willingly the sparse inventory of events he kept in his Day Books towards the end. Though his body had begun to fail him – after a long, driven life of austerity and production – the acuteness of his mind had not diminished a whit.

She had been working on the transcription of the Day Books, and had reached the last but one year of her father's long life. Her habit was to trace the letters alongside, on a separate large sheet of paper. If she kept her eyes half closed and let her spirit enter his, imitating the movements of his hand, she arrived at an enlarged version, blurred at the edges and unravelling; the process reminded her of lying on her back in the sun at the seaside, watching summer clouds spool far above in a strong land breeze, with the signifying shapes captured at the very moment of dissolution. It was still a beautiful script, she thought. It struck full chords on the page like a score. She read:

3. v. 82   Mallalieu: Mountain Lion of the Skies, aragonite, perfect; feathers a little damaged, but pouch intact!

Zunita to Geneva

Ingrown toenail lanced

'Nuke Buenos Aires' stickers: will mankind never learn?

Then, there it was, the cross he used, following convention, though he had famously rejected Christianity:

†Katchina

Katchina had been the last of Helen's dogs; the third generation, technically Katchina III, a thoroughbred Chinese Pard, golden-maned and flat-nosed, tall as a standard poodle, with a terrier's cheerfulness and grit, and a low playful growl like purring.

Zuni Lavery lifted her head and looked up, out of the window; the japonica in the hedge was laden with plump, soapstone-green fruit. Once they had turned yellow, her father had liked to bring them indoors to scent his study with their ripeness; there was a last bowl still standing on his desk, but the fruits were crabbed now, more like raisins to look at than the smooth orbs he'd sniffed at and fingered with such pleasure. He'd always abhorred florists' offerings: 'Never cut the thread of life,' he'd say, 'whatever the organism.'

Her glance lifted across the hedge, and she saw a young woman, with a small rucksack swinging off one shoulder, crossing the road and stopping in front of the sign which gave the opening times of Augustus Lavery House. Today was Tuesday, the Museum was closed; Zunita Lavery sighed. Why didn't visitors read guide-books more carefully? Why didn't people ring up before making the pilgrimage? She'd made sure the tape was switched on this morning, when she got up.

She bent back to the Day Book. The young woman would be disappointed.

The Falklands War had brought her father low; he had been convinced that imperial passions were fading, the only good aftershock of the Nazis' powerlust. 'War fever, again,' he'd groaned when she read him the leaders thirsting for vengeance, the gloating reports of the torpedo hits, the drowned recruits.

She moved on, annotating the text in the margin of her own sheaf of manuscript: 'ZL (that was herself) attended the third Geneva conference of KER, as the representative of AL, whose health did not permit him to travel.'

She had given a paper on behalf of her father to

the delegates from fourteen countries, including a five-
man contingent from Japan, the first time the country
had sent representatives to KER, though the branch
there was now one of the most lively in the world. She
and Gus had collaborated on the topic, 'Orphic gnosis:
embracing the beast within'; she had drafted something
under headings he had given her, and as she read out
her first thoughts to him, he had dictated, thinking
aloud, and then she'd elaborated the arguments and
read the text to him, and he had commented in turn,
expanding and clarifying.

The work exhilarated her as much as if they had
practised a duet together, scrambling after the notes,
losing the beat, and now and then cheating on a passage
and then finding, at last, that they could play it through
in one long breath, and tired and aglow, after the last
chord, put down their instruments. Her father had
been marvellous to work for; always open to sugges-
tion, always glad of a turning her mind might take.
She could see him still, lifting his narrow, eagle-like
head with its sharp crest of white hair and stammering
his pleasure at something she had said, 'That's g . . .
g . . . good, that's very good.' With his curled arthritic
hands joined together in a *namaste* in her direction.

Mallalieu: she would refer the reader back to an earlier page, where the dealer had already been identified.
A man of rare expertise, in her father's opinion; he'd
been an abundant source of gems and amulets, fetishes
and lead pilgrim badges of the type her father could
not resist. He had come round soon after his death, and

made enquiries about her financial affairs. If she was in
any difficulties . . . She'd always suspected Mallalieu
wasn't entirely above board. 'I'll give you whatever
Gus paid in the first place, my dear,' he'd offered.
'Because I have a sense of justice and he was a great
man, indeed, but you know, he was almost the only
collector for this kind of cultic *objet*, and I'm not at all
sure I could move them again for the same amount.
We aren't living in an age of faith, alas, my dear Zuni.'
She couldn't write any of this in the footnotes, of
course, although she knew that her father had been
ahead of his time in his love of Hopi and Navajo and
Zuñi artefacts. As for the Roman gems, she'd seen
inferior hoards in the cases of the best museums.

No, Mallalieu was not going to practise any of his
wiles on her. Gus had been naive, really; unworldliness
was part of his genius, one of his supreme qualities.
Besides, she was his collaborator, the heir and custod-
ian of his thought, and the range of animal symbolism
in the gems – the rock crystal griffins bearing fish aloft,
the haematite wyverns brandishing flails – these and
others had not been properly studied. Lavery scholars
could continue this work of decipherment. Her father
had himself concentrated on the Zuñi fetishes; their
symbolism could never be fully plumbed, he'd declared, they wove a new chain of being to replace
worn-out hierarchies: the Mountain Lion, the Spirit of
the Knife-Plumed Wings, the White Bear and the Black
Bear, the Ground Owl and the Prey Mole and the
Land Snail, the Long-Tailed Wildcat and the Crowned

Eagle. Such totem creatures were carved from shell or antler, jasper and chalcedony as well as other stones and then bound about with feathers and arrowheads and speartips. Sometimes they were hollowed out, and a fine organic dust, the ashes of their tutelary animal spirit, was still preserved inside them, as in a vial; sometimes the pouch in which they had been carried by their former owner, at the belt of a hunter or round the neck of a medicine woman, had not perished, or been lost, as in this example Mallalieu had sold her father. The most prized kind, however – by the Zuñi themselves as well as by Augustus Lavery subsequently – were stones which, in their natural state, resembled guardian animals. 'If only man could do what nature does, without thinking! When consciousness not only disappears as interference to the workings of the spirit, but actually ceases to have being as such at all,' Augustus Lavery would say, and he would stroke Katchina and ruffle up the scruff of her neck, which she enjoyed almost like a cat, and tug at her thick marmalade-coloured coat.

Katchina III had had problems with her kidneys – her death had been expected. But it was still a blow; when Zuni had come back from Geneva and the dog hadn't been there, drowsy in her basket but ready to push herself to her feet and pad heavily to brush against her mistress's knees, Zunita Lavery herself tasted fine sour dust in her mouth like the amulets'. Though Helen had already been gone six years.

She had been Helen's animal familiar, Zuni thought,

not for the first time, and smiled to herself. Gus had always maintained the sympathy of all living creatures. 'What a barbarous creed Christianity is, to deny animals a living soul! Why, a Stone Age hunter had sufficient awareness to perform propitiatory rites in honour of the creature whose death gave him life. He at least could grasp the closeness of his prey to the spirit world! But not Descartes, not the great men of the enlightenment. Oh, no. They thought a dog was a machine.'

After her father died, she'd bought a puppy with a pedigree that overlapped here and there with Katchina's line. She was now adding Mitzi's combings to the bag that had held Katchina's sparse last sheddings. The hair of the breed was soft, like alpaca, durable and strong as spider's thread, and Mitzi's was a delicate tangerine, lighter than Katchina's had been. It would make a fine wool, and she could have it knitted by someone, for a throw rug or maybe even a cardigan. The one Helen made her was long past its best, even she had to admit.

The doorbell rang. Couldn't the young woman read? She was probably Japanese; Zunita hadn't seen her very clearly. She wouldn't answer.

She turned the page of the ledger to the following day,

4. v. 82   Dream: a tree growing from my navel. A nut tree, too! Woke up, laughing.

The bell rang again. Downstairs, Mitzi barked at

the shadow through the glazed sunrise on the front door of the Edwardian house.

Annabel Peake hitched her rucksack from one shoulder to another and glanced up at the house, looking out for movement in any of the windows. She knew the place was officially closed on Tuesdays, she had been there the week before, on a reccy. The attendant had told her that the Archive and the Library were open every day for visitors but that Dr Lavery liked to have one day in the week to herself, since it was still her home. Nothing moved in the leaf-fringed windows; past the edge of her umbrella, she saw tentacles of climbing hydrangea creeping over the sign:

Augustus Lavery 1896–1984
Thinker and Philanthropist
Lived and died in this house
1945–1984

Come on, Dr Zunita Lavery, she prayed to herself, please come to the door. Please, come to the door. She willed it with all her might, and hearing the dog bark, gave another press to the bell, but not for too long. She didn't want to appear pushy.

Her car was round the corner; she'd nearly driven up and parked next to the house – it was the kind of prosperous suburb where commuters lived who had reserved spaces in garages at work, and parking was abundant in the daytime. But she'd thought better of it and, in spite of the showery day, had driven past so that both the smart model and its telltale recent registration

plates wouldn't be connected with her by anyone looking out from Augustus Lavery House. She really
wanted to get this story; at the editorial meeting that
morning she'd volunteered, because she – and several
others – could feel the ground shifting under their feet,
what with the magazine losing nearly £100,000 a week
and the change of editor. The new woman in the job,
Simone Malley, had come in from a men's quality
monthly and was clearly bent on making her mark in
what was a new challenge for her: the weekly supplement of a general readership mass circulation newspaper. From her first morning at work she had been
probing the staff, ready like a grocer to pick out the
fruit with soft spots and bruised bits and throw them
into a box of seconds to trade with market stall owners
at half price. Annabel wasn't going to be one of the
rejects, not if she could help it, not in the present climate when half her friends were already out of work.

There was a footstep inside, and the sound of a voice
hushing the dog. Annabel closed her brolly, mussed
up her hair, and gave a tug at her shirt to loosen it
from the belt. She wanted to look casual, a psychology
student, a recent poly graduate, young and ingenuous.
When the door opened, Mitzi ran out and put up her
muzzle to sniff at the young woman's crotch. Involun-
tarily, Annabel fended off the dog with an awkward
crossing of her legs and an instinctive lowering of her
bag and umbrella to shield herself. Zunita Lavery gave
a small chuckle, realising the girl had her period.

So, to put her more at ease, she called Mitzi to her

and spoke gently. 'Mitzi won't hurt you. It's nature – she has her brains – or some of her brains – in her nose, you see. But your recoil is a natural reaction, too, and one I rejoice in thinking any intruder shares. With a Chinese Pard at my side, I need no protection!'

'Oh, no,' said Annabel. 'I like dogs – it's just that I'm not used to them, and anyway, he doesn't know me, I suppose.'

'She,' insisted her involuntary hostess, for in the exchange Annabel had stepped into the hall and was looking for a stand in which to stow her umbrella. 'We're closed today, I'm afraid,' Zunita Lavery continued.

'Oh no, I thought . . . I've come from . . .' Annabel stammered and her face crumpled.

There was a pause. Then Zunita Lavery relented, and pointed to the hall table. 'You'd better sign the book.'

Annabel brightened, her eyes beamed gratitude, and Zuni, compressing her lips, picked up the Visitors' Book to read her entry. 'Not with an institution, Miss Bolton?'

Annabel gave a little, apologetic laugh. 'No baggage,' she replied. 'No fancy initials after my name. I'm just, well, me. Just me.' She had a naturally girlish voice; usually, she tried to avoid sounding gushy, and cursed its eagerness. But on this occasion she was glad of it; she was gambling that a show of innocence would tell with Zunita Lavery.

'I see you've come from Bury St Edmunds,' she was saying. 'Most of our visitors are Americans. From universities with the names of toothpaste or soap. Americans like to put their name to their works. The equivalent of family tombs. We here believe in leaving a less material trace. Did you take the train?'

'Yes. The directions were spot on.'

'So you did listen to the tape – and you didn't hear that we are closed on Tuesdays?'

Annabel looked down, hitched her bag uncomfortably down from her shoulder and swung it against her legs. 'I must have missed that, I'm sorry.'

'It doesn't signify,' said Zunita. 'You can visit the house on your own; you'll have to do with me as your guide. You'll put up with that. However, I communicate more these days by the pen, and by thought. Never underestimate the power of thought, Augustus Lavery always said.'

'Oh, how wonderful. To have you . . . as my guide,' the young woman exclaimed, and Zunita Lavery basked for an instant. Nevertheless, she concealed her pleasure, asking with some aspersion if Miss Bolton knew who she was, and Annabel Peake responded quickly, brightly that of course she did, that she was Dr Zunita Lavery, that she recognised her from her photographs, that she had read her books.

Her guide, moving towards the door to the first room, off the hall on the right, which Augustus Lavery had used as his study, then declared, with a certain flourish, 'Yes, I am Augustus Lavery's editor and literary executor. He was my father.'

For Annabel the hook was the gay situation. Simone had opened the morning meeting holding up headlined clippings from two dailies: RIOT AT GAY RALLY – 15 HELD. A photograph of men, and some women, was printed underneath. Linking arms, they were facing a squad of police encased in bullet-proof gear, like a plastic tortoise, thought Annabel. Banners above the demonstrators read, 'Restore Our Rights', 'God Loves Gays'. The other clipping reported VATICAN DECREES: GAYS AGAINST NATURE. Simone had then put them down, crossed her legs with a rustle of Lycra hose-clad thigh against thigh, smiled at the staff reporters gathered on easy chairs that placed them below her eye level and asked, 'Anyone remember Clause 28? Anyone heard anything recently about police officers bitten by AIDS carriers? I want this story. I want a *big* story about the state of play in the gay community. I know AIDS charities are bringing in the glamour crowds, that there's nothing more chic than an ACTUP rally, but I think there's another story here, and we're going to tell it. What does it mean to be gay? What are your chances? Are people stopping because of AIDS? What's the deal now for teachers who are gay? Nurses who are gay? Would you go to your dentist again if he came out? Why did Saxon Morris get half a million fucking pounds' damages because the *Despatch* ran the story that he had posed in his birthday suit with a "friend"? Do we or do we not agree with the Pope? He says gays aren't natural – what do we, the British people, think about this?'

Annabel was considered the egghead on the paper's features, because she had an Oxbridge degree in PPP (first-class honours, too) and something about her yappy, well-bred manner provoked her colleagues to tease her. Picking on her braininess came easily to them: she was assigned the job of rounding up comments from the great and the good on Homosexuality Today. 'Get them off guard,' ordered Simone. 'I don't want people watching their backs, toeing the PC line, trying to keep in with everyone. Round up the usuals – the Gay Knights and so on – of course, but branch out. Surprise me.'

When she called the meeting to a close, she detained Annabel: 'Nothing off the record – the barefaced truth – if you can prise it out of them. Use your charms, darling. They aren't exactly negligible.' She gave Annabel a look. 'I've often thought, being gay wouldn't be such a hard life.'

Zunita Lavery was saying, as she turned on the lights in her father's study, 'I'm so glad you came by train. It's the lesser evil, Gus always said. To the motor car. Of course, the bicycle was his favourite means of transportation.'

Annabel stepped into the room. The blinds on the French windows at the end were drawn, and the light from the lamp on the desk and one or two standing on other tables was low. The floor's bare boards were stained the blue of a gull's egg, and covered in part with Navajo rugs; there were strange-shaped rocks positioned here and there, including one which resembled a creature poised for take-off, something between a classical Victory and a Brancuși bird, thought Annabel. She gave a sigh of pleasure and said, inconsequently, 'I took the train because I know cars gave Augustus Lavery the shivers. In fact, I like cycling, too, better than anything. It makes me feel free – the wind in my hair. But now you're meant to wear a helmet. So I've stopped. It's not the same, doing it all encumbered.'

'My dear young woman,' the older woman spoke up sharply, 'Freedom is a more complicated plant than loose hair.'

Annabel was going to say something apologetic, but Zunita Lavery swept on, indicating the desk, on which stood a cluster of animal statuettes, the jade and jasper, cornelian and haematite fetishes of her father's last decade's enthusiastic collecting.

'I'll say a few words, by way of introduction, before leaving you to your own devices, to contemplate and absorb. I'm afraid I shan't draw the curtains, however, just for your visit. It would set off the alarm. You mustn't go past the cord – otherwise we'll have the police here.'

Annabel had read *The World and its Disorders* by Augustus Lavery while she was at university; ever since the lead singer in Up Against It had written the hit song 'Lavery' it had become the cult book of her generation, passing from hand to hand. He was the magus of her cohort; what Gurdjieff had been to the

Twenties, Marcuse and Norman O. Brown to flower power, Popper and Hayek to social Darwinism and the free market, Lavery was proving to be to the apocalyptic, fissile Nineties; just after his death he had been 'discovered' by the young, and become a prophet of psychological ecology, of 'managing' the spirit, of 'getting in touch' with the vitals:

> 'I saw you on TV, Lavery,
> Like a bird up in the sky
> Your thoughts flew so so high
> And I flew with you, Lavery,
> You showed me Natural Ecstasy . . .'

In America at first, then spreading gradually through Europe and reaching, almost last of all, the place of his birth and teaching – London – adepts testified that their world view had been altered by the encounter with his wisdom. After a study weekend devoted to his thought, New York executives returned to their offices and were pleasant to their secretaries, offering to get the coffee for them – or rather the herbal teas they now adopted – and allowing pets at work to keep employees company; Lavery was humanising, it was clear.

'Oh, I wasn't thinking,' Annabel again grovelled, partly in mock-show. 'That was such a silly, thoughtless thing to say. I was distracted, you see, because this is so exciting. I've been wanting to visit here for ages. I'm afraid I'm really glad I'm on my own with you. You must get loads of people usually. When you're open, I mean.'

'Yes, we do,' Zunita replied. The young woman's mouth was mobile, with the fullness and dewy loose-ness of youth; she had pretty hair, fair at the tips of the curls that escaped from the slides with which she had pinned it off her face. 'But some remain invisible,' Zuni went on. She was enjoying having an effect on this callow young person. 'To me, I mean. Now you, you're not invisible. I can see you. You have a definite presence, you seem motivated, and motivation, well used, is energy.' She was looking Annabel in the eye, and Annabel, though the older woman's gaze made her feel as if she were being scraped like some root vegetable for the pot, tried to return it as candidly as possible, rather than betray her duplicity by dropping her eyes. 'Some people are so shrouded in their unful-filled, unspoken longings for this and that that they're more like a big round O, a hunger, not a person. My father . . .'

Annabel remembered something, and quoted, quickly, glad her quick revision of the Lavery books on her shelf before coming had left her a scrap behind: 'The wise man empties himself of all desire, then, like the bellows, he will become full.'

'Aah, yes.' Zunita Lavery gave her visitor a softer, thoughtful look. 'Are you a student? If you are, there's a reduced rate, by the way. £2.00. All proceeds to the Foundation. We do have to pay for –' she waved an arm at the room and at the house beyond – 'the Archive, the Library, unfortunately. I don't like com-merce, but it's necessary to survive.'

'I'm not . . .' Annabel could not manage yet another bald lie, but was reluctant to yield the advantage student status might grant her. 'Well, in a way, studying never comes to an end, does it? I haven't brought my card. Stupid old me.'

'Tsst. Do you think we inspect them here, like bus conductors? You can give me the money later. I should have taken it at the door but I forgot. It's not my usual task, you know.' She paused, then asked, 'Come. You were quoting . . .'

'Your father . . . I'm a real fan, you see, a fully paid-up member of the Augustus Lavery Fan Club.'

'Those weren't his words, you realise.'

'What?'

Zuni encouraged her to remember, with a twitch of her eyebrows.

'No? I thought . . . Whose are they, then? I read it in . . .'

'An epigraph. In *The World and its Disorders*, yes. But my father had many sources. The bellows – the image of the bellows – how beautiful it is!'

Annabel genuinely liked it, too; and was feeling wonder and scorn come at her in waves, alternating to modify the feelings Zunita Lavery's presence inspired in her. Wonder, at finding herself standing in the famous old lion's inner sanctum with his almost equally famous daughter beside her, talking about him; scorn because it had been so much easier than she had anticipated. You could never get a quote from Dr Zunita Lavery; her office never put through calls from the press and she did not answer their letters but passed them on to the Foundation, who sent a routine acknowledgement and an old issue of the KER bulletin. During her father's lifetime they would give press conferences together; indeed, Annabel knew Zunita's small, powerful face from group photographs of KER gatherings as well as from pictures taken of her speaking at such meetings in those days. The young Zunita had been dark-browed, with a slight strabismus, a stubborn jaw and a wilful mouth; the once dark and frizzy shingle of her youth was now white and sparse, and pulled back into a knot at the nape of her neck.

But demand for Lavery's *obiter dicta* had not been as great, then; it began growing slowly, alongside his cult, during the last five years of his life, and apace since his death. Zunita's subsequent reclusiveness, coupled with the constant appearance of new, uncollected work by Lavery under her editorship, had increased the radiance of the nimbus that clothed the almost mythical figure of Gus Lavery in the popular mind.

For there was a rumour underlying his fame, an aspect of his life and character that provoked widespread admiration and even envy among the polished urban high achievers who tempered themselves by weekends in Lavery's posthumous company: that the magus had been wonderfully endowed. Not in anything vulgar like hang or size, but in skill and understanding of pleasure. It was indeed suspected that his régime, however unworldly and ascetic it appeared to be, promoted the required hormones – though Lavery

would never have used such a physiologically deter-
minist argument. He invoked hypnagogic image
identification, summoning up the *nahual*, or animal
familiar most attuned to the individual's character; he
advocated tapping the spinal fluid, raising kundalini – a
yoga term he had incorporated in his eclectic philo-
sophy.

But Lavery's teachings were not orgiastic; he had
also taught restraint, and stressed the value of sexual
containment. Animals mated only to perpetuate the
species; for this reason, Lavery's thought also
interested the Family Values movement. This was why
Annabel had suggested that she try to include the
Lavery angle in the report on Homosexuality Today,
and the reason that Simone had gone for her idea with
such enthusiasm.

'The image of the bellows – it appears first in the *Tao
Te Ching*,' Zunita was explaining. Annabel looked at
her. In her sixties, she had become paler all over, and
the once-etched outlines of her features had been scum-
bled. The effect was altogether less alarming than
Annabel had expected. Furthermore, she was only
around five-foot three, neat and precise and controlled
in her movements, with something of a wind-up doll's
gliding motion, so that Annabel's own coltish limbi-
ness became almost mannered next to her. Only the
slight misalignment of Zunita Lavery's eyes remained
disconcerting.

'Beautiful,' cooed Annabel. 'The contradiction,
between emptiness and fullness.'

Zunita Lavery waved, with a precise gesture, at the room. 'This was my father's study, as I'm sure you've realised. It is exactly as he left it. Except that he would throw open the windows, whatever the season – he loved air, the garden, nature in all her moods. The English climate was the best in the world, he was fond of declaring. It was a way of teasing, too, do you know. But in a way, he believed it. As for me, I'm *frileuse* – I feel the cold. But he wasn't, he didn't understand it, he used to laugh at my cardigans.'

'Oh, I was just thinking,' said Annabel. 'I wonder where she got that fantastic cardy. Where did you get it, by the way? If you don't mind my asking. I love it.'

Zuni plucked at it, almost caressingly. 'It's a very old friend, this one. It was made for me. I can't knit. But I had a friend who enjoyed knitting, it helped her relax.'

'I wish I could! You'd pay – gosh – I don't know, upwards of a hundred quid for something like that now. It's crafts, it's fashion, high fashion now. Does your friend sell them anywhere? She could make a bomb, I'm sure.'

'Helen would be glad to hear you say so. But no. Actually, it's made of . . .' Zuni faltered, and decided against telling the young woman about Katchina's hair. Yet she wanted to talk to her, about Helen. She went on, 'She – that is, my friend, Helen, liked to make her contribution, and she never felt it was enough, though. She sometimes felt . . . a bit of a castaway, I suppose. She never did sell them.'

'I'm sorry. But a castaway – how re
to be a castaway, not to have to accept th
– the hand I've been dealt . . .'

'Well, I'm sure you won't, not if you can he

'To throw it in, start again, new person, ne
new family! I can't tell you how much I – people
age – envy and admire you and your father and . .
people like your friend – who was it? – who were
so bold and broke with convention and braved the
world.'

'My dear, you make it sound so melodramatic. How
Helen would laugh!'

'By the way, Helen . . . is that Helen Copping?'

'Yes: our assistant. On the *Selected Letters*.'

'I know. Gosh, to think she could knit as well!'

'You young women of today. You'll be telling me
next that mending socks is part of the mystery women
have lost.'

'Ugh, no. Not that too?'

'No, not that. We drew the line at socks.'

Annabel smiled and Zuni found herself, to her surprise, twinkling back. But when Annabel began
moving towards the desk in the centre of the room,
Zunita Lavery checked her, 'No further – as I said, the
room is wired. Mitzi knows – she never goes through
the beam. It's not burglars we want to deter, not
exactly. No, it's the souvenir hunters. Do you know,
someone once took the coverlet off Gus's bed – stuffed
it in their handbag, and took it home to . . . who
knows what? Like a comfort blanket, I suppose.'

I still can't believe I'm here. It's . . . it'll sound absolutely fatuous, I know, but it's really as if he had just stepped out of the room. I can feel his presence.' Annabel paused, closed her eyes. 'I just wish I could make the feeling last.' She opened them again, and asked, 'Would he really keep the windows open – on a day like today?'

'He had inner resources, far beyond what you – what people like you and me – can know.'

'But what does that mean? What was that like? To live with, I mean. Wasn't it hard for you all?'

'Us all?' Annabel noticed she was suddenly prickly. She must take care not to alert her – Gus's prowess was dangerous ground, she could see. 'There was only me. And Helen. We looked after his work. And the School, when it was in its heyday – you've been there too?'

'Soon, I want to go, soon. You see, I'm trying to be a writer. I could learn there, I know, so much – '

'A writer? What kind of writing? Never let inspiration pass by. Seize it by the scruff of the neck, and hold on.'

'You were saying, about your father?'

'Yes. It's easy to confuse the freedom of nature – the kind of fulfilment Gus Lavery sought – with licence. They're not the same thing at all. In fact, restraint can prove the greater freedom, he thought. But not restraints like marriage, or mortgages. He moved on light feet.' She gestured at the animals on his desk. 'Like the Mountain Lion. To experience love and to suffer passion are very different things. One is . . .

well, the summit of human aims. The other is disorder, folly, and leads only to grief. One's own and others'. Gus Lavery understood love in the fullest sense.'

'And that didn't mean . . . permissiveness?'

'That's right. Of course, the race has to go on. Though sometimes one does wonder.' She smiled, into the distance. 'No, he wanted to move to nature's rhythm, to find nature's way. He was opposed to the human and all its perversions. To lack of moderation. To compulsion. He wanted to free people from their . . . chains. He did not hold with the slavery of love. Desire is bondage. But he had an appetite for life, you know. And he loved people who had one to match.' She leaned in closer and looked up at the taller, younger woman. 'Sometimes the two go together – I mean, the natural appetite for life and for . . . love. Yes . . . And they were drawn to him. This house, you know, *hummed* with ideas, conversation, exchanges between like minds.'

Annabel was nodding, enthusiastically. Zunita Lavery, standing so near, smelt of leaves turned over in an autumn wood, a pleasant, composty sort of smell. 'I get absolutely green with envy,' Annabel said, intent now on her objective, 'when I read about groups in biographies like the Bloomsberries, or the Impressionists – they all seemed to know each other and love each other, to be friends, sparking away with ideas and support.' She paused, and came to the point. 'And they all slept around too, men with men, women with women, and they got away with it. What did he think of that? I mean, what do you think of that?'

'My father's thought had a profound influence on the Bloomsberries, as you call them. However he was not *of* them. Their ideas about the responsibility of the state towards the citizen show some of his understanding, of course. As for the Impressionists, they were born far too long ago. You must think I'm ancient.' She was almost playful.

'Oh no! You don't look ancient at all. You look . . . wonderful, distinguished, wise. I'm just a peabrain, I'm afraid.' There was a pause, and Annabel, feeling she was wearing the heaviest-duty Doc Martens with metal toecaps, stepped in once again. 'The Impressionists weren't at all gay, were they? Not like some of the Bloomsberries.'

'Thank goodness *he* isn't alive to hear the word used in this way.' She was answering the question, at last, Annabel realised. 'Gus liked so much the idea of *le gai savoir* – gay wisdom – and he certainly did not consider homosexuality either gay or wise. He understood it, the struggle, the torment . . .'

'What do you mean? Surely there's no harm in it, it's just street talk, you know, slang.'

'It's a perversion of meaning, a dreadful falsehood. Gay! Language guards our liberties, it has to be cared for, like anything else.'

'So you think Gus – Augustus Lavery, I mean – would have been upset by the . . . you know, the recent developments? I mean, what would he think

about the Pope declaring homosexuality unnatural on
the one hand, and on the other, gay representatives in
official capacities here and there, government money
spent on gay broadcasting, gay help-points, gay cen-
tres? There've been all these demos – and counter-
demos – I mean, what do you think he would have
thought?' She was breaking the first rule of interview-
ing: Ask one thing at a time and get a straight answer.
'I mean, would he have liked all this, or would he have
been upset by it?'

'Really, young woman. My father was interested in
larger questions, not in a lot of fuss about . . . gratifi-
cation. He would not have been "upset". It took a
great deal to "upset" him – he was a sage, and sages
have discovered peace, at a level the likes of you and I –
and others out there – can never attain.'

'But you must have reached the same level. Surely
you did, being so near him all his life and helping him
with his life's work. No?'

'I . . .' She turned away; something about the young
woman's pressing ardour was agitating her.

'Oh God, now I've put my foot in it. Annabel Peake,
you take the cake.'

Zunita Lavery collected herself. 'Not at all. You
have nothing to do with it.' She had noticed the change
of name. It wasn't entirely unusual for people who
were fascinated by KER to assume a false persona on
first contact. The best disciples did not want to yield
totally, from the start. It was the unconsidered enthusi-
asts you had to avoid; they were the shallow ones.

When Helen first arrived, she'd pretended she wasn't married, she'd used her maiden name. It was only afterwards that she admitted she'd run away from her husband, when she felt they would accept her, and help her keep out of his clutches. As they had done.

She began leading Annabel out of the room, and across the hall, to another room in the house. 'There's a study alcove here, with more materials about Augustus Lavery, if you'd like to look. There are some albums, for instance, which might interest you.'

Annabel followed her, and standing beside her, leaned over to look at a page of snapshots. She was confused; she had become two people, and she detested herself for her pretence. She wished she could suddenly confess, confide in this quiet, grey old lady, tell her about Simone and the *Post*, bring her in to help her clean up her life, be like her. Deal boards, a dog, fruit in bowls, a life of learning and meditation. She bit a strand of her hair, and looked with Zunita Lavery at the album.

Augustus Lavery, with a striped blanket over his knees, was sitting under a lime tree in the garden. 'That's the seventieth birthday portrait. Fine, isn't it?' She paused. 'Helen was also a very good photographer; he didn't know she was taking it. He didn't like being photographed.'

How did someone like Helen Copping become part of a charmed circle? How did other people achieve interesting lives? Annabel wondered.

'Helen was our very first American,' Zunita began,

as if she had heard Annabel. 'She arrived to learn from Pappi – from Gus – during the war. Very soon, we became friends.' Zuni turned a page and again pointed, 'This was the conference, in Rapallo, in 1980.' There was a pause. Then she said, 'That's me in the background.'

Annabel looked: standing behind her father's right shoulder, her deep-set eyes patches of shadow in her small, fierce face, Zuni Lavery did not look at the camera, but askance. 'I'm wearing a very beautiful dress.' She tapped the photo: 'That collar's Neapolitan lace. Pappi chose it, even though it was made by nuns, whose lives perverted the ways of nature, in his view.' She bent to the page, and took her finger off the image.

'And there's Helen's shadow, on the ground, taking the picture.'

Abruptly, she left the table and walked away, through the room, to face across the hall to the entrance to her father's study. Annabel could see her shoulders were quivering; again she pulled a strand of hair into her mouth and nibbled it, embarrassed, impatient, yet gratified, too, at the older woman's commotion.

Zuni took a deep breath. 'At my age, really. Ridiculous, getting upset.' She was half-talking to herself, then raised her voice as she regained control. 'Yet it's surprising how, as the years go by, feelings don't fade. They can even get stronger.' She turned round, and looked at Annabel. 'It's something about today. Something I read in the Day Books. And then your visit. It's come back, all of a sudden, like a piece of music that one hears in one's head, as clearly as if it were being played in front of one. You've brought her back, somehow. She was young too, when she first arrived. And enthusiastic. And she adored Pappi, so much. No, I never managed the peace Gus taught. I struggled to. He helped me, he listened, he understood. But she was my friend.'

The encounter was becoming far more intense than Annabel could cope with, she wasn't made for doorstepping, for these private revelations strangers disclosed to strangers – everyone said that's what happened in journalism, that people were so lonely they'd pour it all out to anyone who cared to listen. But when it was someone like Augustus Lavery's daughter, it was a bit taking aback, to say the least. But she still coaxed, in a tone she hardly recognised as her own, 'What happened? Did she . . . did she leave?'

'Yes, Helen left. We never knew how, or where, or really why she went. She chose to cease to be part of our lives. That's what Papp – what Gus said, at the time. But I . . . I was inconsolable. You young people, you can never understand. When you're young, you think every experience is easy, another will come that will be better. But it's not so. Some things are rare . . . and never come again.

'When I see someone like you, I want you to seize . . . to use . . . your strength. I always suffered from something Pappi called Wanting to Have Something of My Own. He didn't approve.'

'You – your father, I mean – you're quoted everywhere now.' Annabel was trying to bring down the temperature of the exchange. 'Lavery's the absolutely latest buzz word, more than ever, you know. Everyone wants to know what Lavery would have said, done, thought, about this, and that.'

'Buzz word? Ah yes, the press.' She raised her eyebrows, the scorn she felt made her feel better; contempt was a powerful corrective to grief. 'The press always gets things wrong. That's why I refuse to comment. I never give interviews. They understand nothing. Yes, he's recognised. At last. You sound surprised.' She gathered herself together. 'I can't imagine why. If you want to browse, I shall leave you. Come, Mitzi, come.' She had conceded enough; she was tired. The dog's nails skittered on the deal boards in her alacrity to follow.

Annabel was suddenly pleading, 'Oh no, don't go. Please. I'd far rather talk to you. I mean, I can look at the albums later. I didn't mean to sound surprised. It's only that well, it is a bit surprising when the English recognise . . . genius. I mean they usually give the cold shoulder to intellectuals, don't they? I always think people are secretly jolly pleased when one of them brain-drains to America. That sort of thing's all very well for them, they think, or for the French, or the Germans. You and your father and Helen – you don't seem English. Not *English* English. You're different, special. Please, I'd like to write something about this . . . this meeting with you. May I?'

'I'm old. I'm sere.' She paused, she looked at her

visitor. Again, something that had lain quiet inside her was disturbed. 'I was possessive about Helen, Pappi was right. I had to learn . . . and then, well, it was too late.'

'I want to be a writer more than anything.'

'I did too, when I was your age. Creativity is such a precious gift. Yes, yes, do. Try. Write something down. It's a good exercise, you know, of memory and of the heart – KER, the heart. But you know that.'

'You're lucky. No, not lucky. You are what you've made yourself . . . And without you, he wouldn't get half the attention he's getting. People never give the right people their due. I mean, think of Tolstoya copying out *Anna Karenina* – three times. By hand.' She paused, then asked, 'Tell me about Helen Copping. And about Pappi.'

The young woman's tones were eager, her expression beseeching. 'Tell me more.'

As she drove off, Annabel determined, she would return to the office, demand an immediate meeting with Simone, flash fiery eyes at her as she resigned, tell her what a rag she thought the paper was, shake its dust from her feet and return to Augustus Lavery House with an apology – and a resolution; she would become Zunita Lavery's confidante and helper, she would tell the true story of the Laverys, but not in a sensationalist way. A serious, compassionate, documented, authorised biography, the kind British letters excelled at; she would win Zunita's complete trust –

and she wouldn't betray it. She would serve her selflessly, she'd become her amanuensis, as Zunita had been her father's and it would make her – Annabel Peake – respected in her own right; she'd be able to fill in those questionnaires from her old college about what she was doing, instead of staring at the form and not daring to write, Staff Reporter, the *Sunday Post*. 'Biographer, Augustus Lavery' – how much better that would look! He was the genuine article, why, contact with his spirit even when dead and gone to dust had saved her from a worthless life. He was obviously a bundle of complications; like all great men, he was a monster – but what a monster! The excitement he generated was contagious – she was contact-high after only one morning of his daughter's presence. To love a man like that; to be loved by a man like that! Why, one would accept certain conditions. It would be worth it.

She was driving now with one hand, pulling her tape recorder out of the bag with the other.

'Oh fuck, did it work?' She rewound the tape, whipping her hand in the air to make it run faster. As soon as it began slowing down, she stopped it and punched Play. Zunita Lavery's voice rose indistinctly from the small machine: 'Freedom is a more complicated plant than loose hair.'

'I got it!' Annabel beat the wheel in her excitement, saying to herself: 'I got it. I'll show you, Simone Malley, what I'm fucking made of. I thought my jaw would break smiling, but I got the story. And it's beautiful, it's beautiful.'

'How's this for a lead?' She raised her voice over the recording, as if dictating: "The blue eyes of Dr Zunita Lavery filled with tears as she remembered her dear friend – Helen Copping. Zuni lived with Helen for x years, until 19 . . . whatever. But her father, the late sage, drew the line at gay love. The prophet who taught a generation to embrace the beast pointed out that beasts don't . . ." '

Then she thought, Annabel Peake, stop it at once. You were going to pack it in, you were having a change of heart. Lavery would never have found himself on the same side of the fence as the Pope – or let himself be put there. There are oppressors and oppressors, you know that. Besides, admit it, you liked the old witch.

She was resolved; she was destined for heroic deeds; she would become one of the hard and the pure.

Zunita Lavery stood in her father's room. There was one occasion, she remembered, when she had come in and he had been kissing Helen. They hadn't seen her, though he would have been able to then, it was before his eyes failed. Helen had looked blissful, greedy as a baby at the breast, and it was this trustfulness in contact with Gus that had most hurt Zuni. The only time she had been that close to Helen physically was during one of the KER conferences when the hotel gave them a room with a double bed, and she stopped Helen trying to change it. It wasn't that she wanted to make love to her, not exactly, but she wanted to have her near; in the night she watched her, and Helen's habitual air of fussing had not relaxed even as she slept. Zunita had wanted to kiss her, between her eyebrows, to smooth away her worry, but something had failed inside her – she had not dared to.

Then in the morning, Helen had complained that Zuni was incredibly difficult to sleep with, always tossing and kicking and even snoring. But it wasn't true, Zuni knew; it was the strength of her feelings that had penetrated deep into Helen's sleep.

'Did you get the goods?' Simone said, coming out of one of the toilets in the Ladies' room at the *Post*.

Annabel was at a basin washing her hands; she was taken by surprise.

'Yes, I did,' she said. 'I got an interview – it was a hard slog, but I got it.'

'That's the best kind,' said Simone, pushing the door to leave with a clanging of her gilded costume jewellery manacles. With her free hand, she clenched to demonstrate: 'Squeeze till the pips squeak.'

Zunita Lavery pushed down on the old pain, now. She went to Gus's desk, passing beyond the wire. No alarm sounded. She had deceived the young woman about that; she would always resist impiety. Nobody could just walk in off the street and come close enough to her father's things to touch them. Not even someone who reminded her of Helen. She bent to tousle Mitzi's mane, and the dog gave her purry growl in response.

She would return to work now, in her own study, and continue deciphering the Day Books; her father's thought needed her vigilance. She paused, then picked up the wizened quince and sniffed them: dust. She would throw this old fruit away and wait for the new crop to ripen and refresh the bowl.

Available from Vintage

by

Marina Warner

INDIGO

'A complex, glittering book'
The Times

'An extraordinary imaginative achievement'
Times Literary Supplement

JOAN OF ARC

'This is a profound book, about human history in general and
the place of women in it, as well as about a fifteenth-century
heroine. No one, I think, could read it without being the
better for it'
Christopher Hill, Sunday Times

IN A DARK WOOD

'Marina Warner's prose is gracefully analytical, her meanings
are distinct, and the structures of the novel carefully modulated . . .
this is an elegant novel, and it signals a major talent'
Peter Ackroyd, Spectator

THE SKATING PARTY

'Recalls writers like Elizabeth Bowen and Rosamond
Lehmann . . . Marina Warner is a novelist of real talent and
fine discrimination'
Scotsman

VINTAGE